The Package.

A Tale of the Holocaust.

By

Ellen Dudley

and

T. J. Edison.

Acknowledgments.

In this part-fictional story, real-live people are mentioned. Elfriede Mollenhauer and her siblings, Hans and Emil, and Paula who won bronze at the 1936 Olympics, and Robert, who was the first radio sports reporter in Germany, not forgetting her husband Hans Thunsdorff, their son Peter Thunsdorff and his son Claudio, along with Christian Petry, Dr Peter Hasenclever, Kaethe Kollwitz, Ellen Kaempfer, her husband and her sister Betty Holstein, are/were real people - though their words are mainly our own. All other characters portrayed here are a figment of my and my daughter's imagination. Elfriede was a member of the communist party, only because this was the better organised resistance movement.

My daughter and I would like to thank Peter Thunsdorff, son of Elfriede and Hans, for his help and cooperation, for providing us with important details about his parents and for his permission to put down in words these facts.

We dedicate this book to, Petra, wife and mother.

We wish to thank Gretchen Steen, author of 'Legend of Dragamere' for her help in formatting, and for her professionally constructed cover designs; without her we would have been lost.

"The fiction in today's writing is becoming more surreal and imaginative, some even very far-fetched, but fiction is just that – to make the unbelievable...believable!"

Gretchen Steen.

http://www.gretchensteen.com/index.html

Author's notes.

"Recollections".

I thought it would be easy to research, translate, and write this book with my father. However, it did not turn out that way. We did not need much of an imagination to describe the terrible and tragic scenes concerning Ellen, her sister and her travelling companions after researching and reading so much about them over the years. He and I had to re-live the persecution, the degradation, the cruel murder with each word, and we felt the desolation, the mental pain and to be honest we were not sorry to finish it. The trouble now is we cannot leave the tears behind.

Ellen Dudley. 2011.

In 1933, persecution of the German Jews became active Nazi policy, but at first laws were not as rigorously obeyed or as devastating as in later years in other countries. On April 1, 1933, Jewish doctors, shops, lawyers and stores were boycotted. Only six days later, the Law for the Restoration of the Professional Civil Service was passed, banning Jews from being employed in government. This law meant that Jews were now indirectly and directly dissuaded or banned from privileged and upper-level positions reserved for 'Aryan' Germans. From then on, Jews were forced to work at more menial positions, beneath non-Jews.

The Nazi persecution of the Jews culminated in the Holocaust, in which approximately 6 million European Jews were deported and murdered during World War II. On May 19, 1943, Germany was declared judenrein - clean of Jews; also judenfrei: free of Jews. It is believed that between 170,000 and 200,000 German Jews had been killed.

"In Germany today it is a criminal act to deny the Holocaust or that six million Jews were murdered in the Holocaust (§130 StGB); violations can be punished with up to five years of prison."

The Package.

A Tale of the Holocaust.

Chapter one.

Hamburg September 1924.

Ellen Kaempfer and her sister Betty Holstein walked amongst fallen leaves as they strolled through Hamburg's *Stadtpark*. Ellen looked back at the two men, following them some distance behind, as one of them laughed out loud.

One of them wore a sailor's uniform, the other expensive civilian clothing. The civilian, named Johannes Kaempfer, '*Henness'* for short, shook his head, ceased laughing. "Where do you get them from, Willy, do you have a book full in your cabin?"

"No, Hanness, I have a good memory, especially for anecdotes."

Ellen turned back to Betty. "Hanness' finds your boyfriend entertaining."

Betty smiled. "Sailors are something special. Willy is a navy man; they are a special breed."

Ellen moved closer. "Has he proposed?"

Betty sighed. "No."

Betty wasn't getting any younger, Ellen hoped this was the right man for her. "Do you like him a lot?"

She nodded, her eagerness apparent. "Of course I do."

Ellen glanced back at the pair, she liked Willy, he was often boisterous but soft spoken the rest of the time. "What about him?"

Betty glanced back. "Well he hasn't mentioned anything about marriage."

"He's a catholic, isn't he?"

"Yes."

"Have you met his parents?"

"They live in Berlin, Ellen, he's only stationed here."

She detected a note of despondency. "He won't be here

forever, will he?"

Another sigh. "I know."

Smiling, Ellen said, "You haven't given in to him have you?"

Betty's brow creased. "Of course not, he's a catholic." She paused, said, "Have you discussed children with Hanness', a family?"

She had discussed children, but Hennes wanted to have a house with a garden. "He wants to buy a house first; you know he has a good job as assistant bank manager. He says he has enough for a house at the moment, but not for furniture."

Betty raised an eyebrow. "Have you looked at any houses?"

"Yes, several."

"And…"

"We want one with a garden, but we haven't been offered one yet."

"Ellen, Betty," said Willy as the two men caught up with them, "How about coffee and cream cake,"

"Good idea," said Betty, "I'm feeling rather peckish."

Betty was dieting, she thought to remind her, saying, "You're always feeling peckish," looking pointedly at Betty's waistline.

"I've lost weight, sister dear," said Betty, which was true.

Willy and Henness' offered the women their arms and off they went. Ellen hugging her husband's arm with Willy chattering ten to the dozen while Betty giggled.

A chance meeting.

Hamburg Jan 24th 1932.

Thirty-five year-old Elfriede Mollenhauer, member of the German communist underground, spotted the man, one of her contacts, a key member of the underground movement, walking towards her from the direction of the railway station. She shivered as the night breeze blew around her calves and through her wavy blond hair. Her gazed drifted past him, searching the faces of the people around him; he was definitely alone, as she knew all of them by sight having met them at one of the security briefings.

Her thoughts went back to her verbal instructions. *'There should be three of them, Helga, Gunter, and him.'* She couldn't see the others. *'Has something gone wrong, if so, what's he doing here?'*

She called out, smiling as she waved, "Hubert, over here," and went to meet him.

They held out their arms as they neared one another, embraced, kissing like lovers. They broke off after a short while. She said, "The show starts soon, come; we're going to be late if we don't hurry." They walked off, her arm in his, she added, "Where are the others?"

He smiled. "They didn't make it in time. I was told to come alone. I thought I'd been spotted on the train. Two Gestapo types were eyeing me for a while. I pretended to doze and snored quietly. I must have been very convincing as they left me alone, picked up a couple of old people and left at the next stop. " He raised his voice, "The sights in Berlin are brighter now that spring approaches."

"I suppose they are," she said, smiling in return, pulling him to her, kissing him on the cheek, their play-acting a necessary precaution.

They approached the theatre, joined the queue. The crowd moved forwards slowly into the foyer. At the entrance to the auditorium, two middle-aged women directly in front of them searched frantically through their handbags. One of them said, "I can't find them. Have you got them?"

Her companion finished rummaging saying, "No. Oh no, I must have left them on the mantelpiece. Oh, what do we do now?"

The other shook her head. "This is your silly husband's fault, him and his bowling club, rushing your evening meal after coming home late, you should have left his meal on the table and come to my apartment."

As they turned to leave, Elfriede took out the extra tickets from her handbag, held them out. "Excuse me, I have two extra tickets, my friends had to call off at the last minute, here, you can have them."

One of the women said, "I'm afraid the tickets were with my purse and..."

Elfriede insisted, "Take them please, as a gift. Besides, we are holding up the queue." She pushed the tickets into the woman's hands; the woman turned to her companion, smiled saying, "Thank you, thank you very much." They moved on. Elfriede and Hubert followed them inside after giving their tickets to the usher.

Once in their seats, she turned to the nearest woman, who

was in her mid-forties. "They were sold out you know, so you would have been out of luck."

The woman smiled, nodded. "Thank you, you are most kind and generous."

"They were a gift," she said, "and it would have been a shame to throw them away, especially for a Verdi opera." She added, "By the way, my name is Elfriede Mollenhauer, I am here with my cousin Hubert, he is from Berlin."

The woman nodded to Hubert, who was listening in. She said, "My name is Ellen Kaempfer, and this is my sister Betty."

The other woman leaned forward, smiling, whispered, "Pleased to meet you, and thank you."

At that moment, the lights went out. Elfriede slipped Hubert the papers he needed for his journey; he stowed them inside his jacket.

After the performance, Elfriede stood in the foyer chatting with several acquaintances; Hubert slipped away without comment with another woman, similar in appearance and dress to Elfriede who waited until they left the theatre ahead of her.

As she arrived on the street, the two women, Ellen and Betty, were waiting for her. The younger one said as she extended her hand, "We would like to thank you; it was very kind of you to give us those tickets."

She took Ellen's proffered hand, felt the presence of a wedding ring under the glove. Elfriede said, "Don't mention it; any friend of Verdi is a friend of mine."

The three of them laughed. Ellen asked, after looking at the people passing by, "Where is your cousin?"

Elfriede shrugged lightly. "Oh, he's gone to a party with friends of ours, they insisted on showing him the town, I unfortunately must work tomorrow."

As they walked on she looked at the pair. Their clothes were not all that expensive but their appearance was neat. She looked at Ellen's sister, who seemed a little nervous, looking away as two police officers walked slowly by.

Elfriede looked behind her then turned saying to them softly, "You are both Jewish aren't you?"

They stared at her and slowed to a stop.

Elfriede held up her hand. "I am anything but a supporter of this government, of this tyrant, this pontificating loudmouth and his cronies," she said, "Why are you still in Germany? It would be safer if you left, for I believe things could get worse."

She saw two police officers approaching, and she turned to Ellen as they walked on. "And the Fuhrer was happy to receive us, as my father said he would be."

Ellen nodded. "They say he is a charming man."

They passed the police officers, Elfriede continued, "Do you know what he said to us about my sister receiving her medal?" As they turned the corner, she turned to the two women, "You two took a chance going to the theatre."

Ellen smiled. "We wouldn't have missed it for the world."

As the reached the end of the street, Betty stumbled, cried out, Ellen caught her, Elfriede came to her side. Ellen said, "It's her Arthritis, her knees, it is getting worse and her Lumbago is acting up again, she needs to rest."

Elfriede thought it would be better to get her off the street. She peered down the road, waved to an approaching taxi; it stopped and she opened the door. Ellen looked at her in surprise as Elfriede took Betty's arm, "Come on. I don't know where you live, so you will have to tell the driver."

Ellen helped her sister inside and Elfriede joined them. Ellen told the driver, "Eichenstrasse 22," riding the taxi in silence.

After a while, Ellen pointed, "We are here now, the last door but one."

As the driver pulled up at the address, Ellen called out, "Just a moment please, I'll go and get my purse."

Elfriede touched her sleeve. "No you won't, you will help your sister, I have to drive on, I have a pressing appointment, until the next time then."

Ellen helped Betty out of the vehicle and took out her door key. As the taxi door closed, she turned and waved to Elfriede and found her smiling as she waved back.

***

Elfriede sat across from Kurt, her controller, in the empty café, nursing a cup of coffee. He said, "Yes, I heard they had to split up, but the others are safe, the one you delivered is very important to the movement, you did well."

The entrance door opened, an elderly couple entered. He glanced around at them casually, waited until they sat at the other end of the room before he said, "Now you must leave the group, forever, forget everything you have heard or seen, if you see anyone from our movement, on the street, just ignore them, if they approach you for some reason, deny quietly any knowledge of your association with them."

Stirring her coffee, she asked, "Don't you trust me?"

He was silent for a short while as he stared down at the table top. Then he surprised her as his eyes met hers, "I would trust you with my life."

She saw truth in his features, she saw the moistness in his eyes had increased and her heart warmed to him. She thought about Ellen and Betty. "What is going to happen to the Jews here in Germany?"

He shrugged heavily, "I really don't know, Molli, but I have a sense of foreboding that the Nazi's are cooking something up. Many young Jewish men and women are with the resistance here in Hamburg, they will not leave, their parents and other relatives have left for other lands, what will happen to those remaining I have no idea. I suspect Hitler wants to control the whole of Europe, and anybody who believes he doesn't is a fool. We know he will move on Poland, we have told our counterparts over there, but they say Hitler is a little man with a big mouth who is afraid of the Russian Bear."

She emptied her cup. "Yes, he is, but he is evil and deceitful and he has a vast army."

"Hitler is afraid of Ivan and wants the British as his Allies, they, and the French want peace in Europe, but the French have their own problems, just like Spain, and the Americans are contently sitting on the fence while watching the sideshow, probably taking bets."

"Are we talking about war?"

"If Hitler has his way, yes."

"We've only just got over the last one; I don't think Germany is prepared."

"Molli, Hitler has a large modern army and it is growing, he has support in other lands, the whole of Germany is behind him too, there is nothing we can do to stop him, all that we and other resistance cells can do is be the proverbial fly in the ointment, nothing else."

She hid her despondency and said, "Do you think you could

get two female friends of mine a visa, Britain or America?"

"They are Jewish I presume."

"Yes and I don't think they are all that well-off."

He drained his coffee cup, "Britain will not be a safe place for them if Hitler invades, America or Canada would be better, but it's getting late for there now, German Jews aren't the only ones trying to find a new homeland, and I suspect the worse as far as all Jews are concerned, things could turn nasty for them and other 'non-Aryans' here quite soon." He paused for a while, "I will not promise anything, but I will try. It will be difficult and will take some time, if you give me their details I will see what I can do, if I am successful I will need photos."

She twisted a serviette in her hands, "And when you can do nothing, what then do you suggest?"

"Pray, pray to God that my suspicions are unfounded."

Chapter two

Hamburg, June 1933.

Ellen.

Ellen and her sister Betty descended the synagogue steps. Ellen looked up at the sky, smiling. "It looks like we are in for warm weather today," she said.

"Just the weather for my knees, the winter was bloody awful, rain, rain, nothing but bloody rain," said Betty as they stepped down onto the pavement.

While walking arm in arm through the suburbs on their way home, they saw the apartment blocks, the pavements before their entrances scrubbed clean, the gutters freshly swept. Strangers passed them, exchanging greetings, several with a Nazi salute and a loud 'Heil Hitler' which they returned with a smile, something they had quickly gotten used to doing.

They, like all Germans, were proud of Germany's new status, a new age had begun. No more starving people, no more jobless and homeless. Adolf Hitler had changed everything for the better and they believed the best was yet to come.

Ellen sniffed the air, "Ah!" she said, "Freshly ground coffee."

They passed a café, it's front window displaying gateau's and pastries. Ellen tugged on Betty's arm before increasing her pace saying, "I do believe Germany is on its way towards a better future," to take Betty's mind off the treats on display.

"I wouldn't be too sure about that. Have you seen those brown-shirted Meschugge, parading with their placards, what have they got against Jews anyway?"

"I'm not sure; I believe they are disillusioned, they are unhappy about something political, something the Fuhrer has yet to put straight."

"Your Fuhrer, as you put it, is more interested in himself after his accomplishments. It seems he wants people to worship him, all this 'Heil Hitler' nonsense. Childish, if you ask me."

As they rounded the next corner they stopped dead in their tracks, regarding the commotion ahead. They stood there, Betty her brow creased, Ellen holding her hand to her mouth as a group of men, dressed in khaki uniforms, ripped items of clothing apart right in the middle of the street. They were accompanied by lookers-on, civilians; some were applauding, urging them on.

Ellen and Betty stood frozen on the spot as they saw a man's three-piece suit, an evening gown fly out from a broken display window, landing on the roadway.

One of the men grabbed the dress, held it up. The gown, a brilliant white, soon joined the mound of clothing, torn viciously in two; the same thing happened to the suit.

Two more men came out of the shop carrying bundles of cloth, which they dropped onto the pile. One of them opened a small can, poured the contents onto it. After he retreated, the other set fire to it, stepping back as the flames leapt up, saying, "That's another load of Jewish shite less to worry about."

Ellen cringed inwardly as another man ran out of the shop, laughing, giggling insanely, throwing items of underwear onto the blaze.

"Not fit for human attire, not even fit for pigs," he called out, which caused the others to laugh as they swaggered off to their waiting vehicle, an open-topped truck, bearing several red, white, and black flags.

Ellen glanced at Betty whose brow was now unclenched as

she stared at the blaze.

As the truck drove off, most of the crowd dispersed. Ellen and Betty walked on towards the clothier's establishment. The sign above it read, 'Silberman and sons.'

Treading carefully over glass shards they saw the shattered shop window; its display stands void of clothing. Four people; a man and woman, accompanied by two boys, stood in the doorway. Ellen recognised the woman, having shopped there a while ago. They stopped, waited, watching while the four edged through the splintered doorway, out onto the glass-strewn pavement, staring at the bonfire.

The man, in his early forties, held a blood-soaked handkerchief to his face, while the woman supported him. The two young boys followed them. One of them, the youngest, about eight years old, tugged his father's jacket. "Why did they do that Papa, why did they hit you and call us those awful names, what have we done?"

The other boy, his features drawn, placed his arm on his shoulder. "It's because we are Jewish, Philipp, nothing more."

The woman glanced at Ellen, smiled sadly, nodded, turned to

her children.

Ellen wondered if she should say something, but at that moment the woman reached out to her children, pulling them nearer to her. "Let us go back inside and pack our things, we are leaving this place," she said, holding her head high.

"Where are we going?" asked the youngest child.

The woman took hold of her injured husband's arm and said, as she led them back towards the doorway, "Far away, my son, as far away as possible."

They disappeared inside the shop. Ellen's heart was racing, she felt a little faint. Betty took her arm pulled her to her. She took several deep breaths, walked on with her past the opening, not daring to look inside.

They passed several onlookers who were talking, laughing amongst themselves, commenting on the occupants, saying they were lucky not to be beaten up. The scene troubled Ellen; why had these people condoned such activities, why had nobody called the police?

She wondered why Germany's new leader allowed such a thing to happen. She turned at the silence, saw the onlookers observing them. A chill ran down her spine.

When Betty tugged on her arm she turned her gaze away, feeling insecure all of a sudden. After they turned the next corner they increased their pace.

"So much for your Adolf," said Betty.

"He's not to blame," said Ellen.

"Didn't you see the swastika?"

"It's a good luck symbol."

"Yes and your Adolf uses it on all his official documents and his flags. Open your eyes sister. I have a feeling that things are going to get worse, not better. In fact, back there, I felt somebody walk over my grave."

Biersdorf.

A black Citroen and a half-dozen army lorries pulled to a halt in the village square in front of the town hall. The car's passenger door swung open, Gauleiter Andreas Gault, overweight, dressed in his khaki uniform, perspiring heavily, heaved himself out. He swaggered over to the small crowd assembled there, stopping a few metres from them. An elderly man stepped forward with his hand outstretched. "Good morning, Herr Gault."

Gault, sent to organize the home guard, ignored the hand. He stared at the man. "What do you mean, 'Good morning'?"

The old man shuffled awkwardly. "Sorry, I meant, good morning, Herr Gauleiter Gault, welcome to Biersdorf."

Gault stepped closer, smacked the man hard across the face with his gloved hand. The old man staggered under the blow. He held his hand to his face, staring at Gault.

Gault raised his voice, "Not 'good morning', you arsehole," he raised his arm, outstretched, saying, "Have you not heard, 'Heil Hitler' is the greeting now, you will raise your arm like this when greeting someone and say with pride, 'Heil Hitler,'" then he dropped his arm, strutted back and forth.

The crowd turned their eyes to the old man, who raised his arm saying, "Heil Hitler."

Gault roared, "I meant everybody."

The crowd muttered, with raised arms, a series of, "Heil Hitler."

Gault screamed, "In unison you pig-dogs, and louder - on my command."

He waved his hand like a conductor, "One…two…three," nodded.

And the crowd shouted, "Heil Hitler." Feeling somewhat relieved when Gault smiled, returning the salute.

"Much better. I hate dissenters."

He turned to the Wehrmacht sergeant and his men, standing by their vehicles. "Sergeant Brinkmann, you can billet your men as designated, I'm off for a beer." He turned back to the crowd, shouted, "Where's the damned innkeeper?"

The NCO called out, "Corporal Schafhausen, bring me the roster." A portly soldier stepped forward with a clipboard.

Brinkmann took it, ran his eyes down the list, "Oberstürmbahnführer von Hutten should be arriving soon. You lot are to control the crossroads outside the village, day and night. The vehicles heading for the work camp have priority; so set up the barriers and the rest of the soddin' paraphernalia, and be quick about it, I want to make a good impression." He winked at, Schafhausen, lowered his voice, "You, Franz, are billeted with family Dorn, a farmhouse on the edge of the village. They have three unmarried daughters; you should do nicely there, good food, plus you know what."

As Schafhausen hurried off, Maria Holding, a local farmer's wife, watched as the fat man in the gaudy khaki uniform swaggered off with Herr Schmitt to the inn. She wondered where her sons, soldiers of the Wermacht were, she prayed daily for their safe return. Then she turned away in disgust as Gault scratched his backside vigorously, before entering the tavern.

Hückelhoven. North-Rhein Westphalen.

A large town near the Dutch border.

Johannes Kirsch called out, "Come in," after hearing a knock on his office door.

Two men dressed in civilian clothing entered, one of them, a scar marring his nose, spoke, "You are, Johannes Kirsch?"

Kirsch nodded, sensing something sinister in the man's tone. The other said, "Get your coat, you are coming with us."

Kirsch rose up, fearing the worst. "What for?" he cried, reaching for his overcoat hanging behind him. "Is it about that article

I published?" The pair regarded him in silence, "I only printed the truth." They stared at him as he said, "I am not a criminal, and I protest."

Scarface glared at him. The other smiled, then said, "Put your coat on, it's going to be a long drive."

"Where are you taking me?"

Scarface's upper lip curled, "Gestapo headquarters, in Aachen."

Kirsch, seated in the rear, looked out of the side window; in the distance he saw another church steeple. He recognised the city it belonged to - Julich, an ancient and picturesque city. He recalled he had a second cousin there, Inga, a young widow from his father's side of the family. She was several years younger; he hadn't seen her since her son's christening. Maybe they would drop him off there on the way back.

He thought about what he'd published in his newspaper, an article about the qualities of leadership, questions on Hitler's rise to power. He assumed they would force him to print a retraction - well he'd be damned if he would.

They drove through a village, it was market day. The driver leaned on the car's horn to clear the pedestrians from the cobbled street.

They left the buildings behind, motored on down a road that dwindled into the distance as Kirsch watched. He looked up at the cloudless sky as the vehicle, a black sedan, pulled to a stop. He called out, afraid, "Why are we stopping here?"

The driver said without turning to him, "Piss-stop, get out."

The man climbed out, closed the car door. Kirsch said, "But I don't have to go."

Scarface nodded, "You do now, so get out, move it!"

Kirsch climbed out with him. The driver said, as he opened his fly, "Just walk over to that bush and relieve yourself, and no funny business, we'll do it by the car."

Kirsch walked off towards a bush some ten metres from the road side, he heard several clicking noises behind him, but he didn't hear the shots that killed him.

Chapter three.

Hamburg 1936.

Elfriede.

Elfriede Mollenhauer stood by the radio, listening to the familiar voice of her brother, a radio announcer *'...and the bronze medal goes to Paula Mollenhauer. My goodness, just listen to the crowd, they are-.'*

Alone in her third-floor apartment, she turned the radio off, and walked away from the sideboard after hearing her twin brother Robert on the radio, one of Germany's first sports commentators, speaking live from Berlin.

Her sister Paula had trained so hard for the discus event. Nevertheless, she herself had refused to go. She wanted no part in this charade; for she knew, the Nazi's were using it mainly as propaganda.

She walked off into the kitchen, there she filled the water kettle, slammed it onto the stove. She lit the gas beneath it, threw the matches down onto the table. She gazed out of the kitchen window muttering, "Damn bloody Nazis."

Hamburg 1937.

Apprehended.

Elfriede strode over to the lounge window, said to her brother, who had decided to pay her a surprise visit, "It's turned awfully dark outside. I think rain is on its way." She pulled back the lace curtain and peered at the heavy clouds. She glanced down at the empty street at the passers-by, saw the black saloon car as it stopped outside her apartment block. "The Gestapo!" She cried.

Emil, her thirty-six-year-old brother, stared at her over his coffee cup as he drained it, his brow creasing.

She stepped back from the window, looked in the direction of her writing desk. "They're coming here, my typewriter, I have to get rid of it," she cried.

His jaw dropped open, he said, "What, you too?"

She visualized the Gestapo comparing her typewriter lettering with illegal leaflets. *'Oh, my God, if they find it they'll match the letters and then-.'*

Without waiting for an answer, Emil placed his empty coffee cup in the saucer, stood up, brushed past her, grabbed her machine from the desk, raced out of the apartment.

Recalling her brother's recent words, she realised they were both working against the Nazi government; she wondered with which group he was with.

She heard him going down the back stairs as she closed the door behind him. She walked into the lounge, gathering her thoughts.

After a short while, she heard the heavy knocking on the door. She took a deep breath, walked across the room, opened it. "Yes, can I help you?"

A tall man, in the typical grey leather trench coat, wide-brimmed trilby, barked out, "Are you, Elfriede Mollenhauer?" Before she could answer, he pushed the door open wider. He gesticulated with a flickering movement of his right hand, followed her, accompanied by two of his colleagues as she walked away from him.

As they came to a stop in the middle of the lounge, she told him, "Yes, that's me" then she asked him, "What is this all about, has something happened?"

He stared at her, his eyes cold, probing.

Breathing slow, deep, she stared back politely with a hint of a smile on her lips.

She heard the other two men wandering about her apartment, searching the rooms, opening, shutting drawers, but she kept her eyes on the man before her. She knew they would never find what they were looking for, as it was not there anymore. Knowing her brother, the typewriter would now be lying at the bottom of the Isebek canal.

The two men returned with several books, handed them to the tall one. He looked at them for a while, flipping through the pages. He showed them to her, "These are subversive literature, communist drivel."

She peered at the books' back covers, her brow lightly tense, after which she shrugged lightly, "I wouldn't know, I haven't read them yet, do you think I should get rid of them?"

He stared intently at her features, as if seeking some hidden humour there as she added, "The books probably belong to one of my friends, I entertain a lot you know."

His eyes bored into hers, he seemed undecided as she smiled back at him, then one of the men came over, indicating. "She's got Kollwitz hanging on her wall."

He turned to where the man was pointing. He turned back to Elfriede, jerked his thumb, "That photo behind me, a friend of yours?"

She looked beyond him at the picture, just before one of the men removed it from its place; it was a photo of her friend Kate, an opponent of the Nazi regime.

She turned back to him, "Kaethe Kollwitz? No, we have never met, why, is there something wrong with it, it was given as a present, a decoration, she's a well-known poet, I've been told?"

He looked her up and down, his eyes cold. "Get your coat," he said, "you're coming with us."

Interrogation.

The car pulled up outside a grey-stone building, she knew it was Gestapo headquarters. She climbed out after one of them, the others followed them into the building, with all of them hurrying as the rain started its descent.

Holding her by the arms, they marched her into the cellar. Their journey took them along a darkened corridor, ceasing each time they stopped to unlock several metal doors, pulling them hard to, the clang echoing into the murky depths, after which they locked them noisily again; showing her there was no chance of escape from this dark and threatening place.

They stopped at a wooden door, one of them unlocked it, bundled her inside a dimly lit room. He brought her to a table, surrounded by several chairs; he pushed her down onto one of them and barked, "Stay there and keep quiet." Then he left, making a show of locking the door after slamming it shut.

She sat for a while in the semi-darkness, the only light coming from the corridor by way of the gap under the door.

She wondered what was to become of her. Had they caught Emil? She hoped to God not, and she thought of what to say in his defence. She took off her heavy coat and hung it over the back of the chair.

After a while, a key turned in the lock, then the door burst open and two men entered. One of them, a head shorter than the other, switched on an overhead light almost blinding her. They sat down at the table across from her. The taller one said, "Place your hands on the table."

Her hands dropped down from her eyes, she looked across the table at the two of them, both wearing their wide-rimmed hats, casting their features in darkness. The light hurt her eyes as she tried to make out their faces, in the end she gave up, looked down at her hands, clasped together on the bare wooden table.

Goose bumps formed on her arms, she shivered slightly after the shock of the seizure had worn off. She began to feel the cold, sitting there in her short-sleeved blouse and skirt, keeping her breathing even, hiding her anxiety.

The short one rose up, strode over to the radiator; he turned the knob to its maximum then returned to his seat. After several seconds pause, a familiar voice spoke out harsh and loud, startling her, "So you are Elfriede Mollenhauer?"

"Yes," she said remaining calm.

"Look at me when you answer."

She looked up immediately, all she could see was their clothing, their faces, still in black shadow.

The other said shortly after, almost inaudibly, amidst the ticking of the radiator, "We have a few questions about your activities and your associates." He added peevishly, "And you will answer truthfully or face the consequences."

The room's temperature had increased, the air was thick, and she could smell their sweat in the hot, stuffy room. They had been at it for hours, always the same questions, some quick-fired, others with pauses in between, without a mention of Emil. She wondered who would give in first, hoping to God it would not be her.

She knew the tall one from his voice, but the other was a stranger; his voice being somewhat effeminate, his manner of questioning bordering on petulance when he lisped.

The one she knew now slid a photo agonisingly slow across to her, asked, "This man is a known opera fan; you may have seen him at the opera house you visit, have you seen him recently."

She looked at the man in the photo, of course she knew him, but not from the opera house. He was her controller, she had never spoken to him in public, she never would do. They would approach one another on a certain street at alternate times, if he paused, looked down purposefully at one of his shoes, she would go to her Post Box, a certain hollow tree in the local cemetery. There she would receive a coded message as to where to find her instructions, passed on, on a tram journey or in a certain Taxi on a certain street at a designated time.

She took a deep breath and answered, "No."

"Do you know a man named Kurt Wellenbach?"

"No."

"What about Andrea Kaspers?"

"No."

"Kaethe Kollwitz?"

"I know of her."

"So you said."

"You had her portrait on your living-room wall."

"Yes, it was a Christmas present."

Silence reigned for a short period, the two men whispered inaudibly amongst themselves, as the radiator ticked loudly.

One of them slid another photo across the table, "Have you seen this man," he paused and showed her another two photos, "… with this man, … or with this woman?"

She answered each question, "No!"

They presented dozens more photos, showed her some of them repeatedly in the hope of confusing her, she would tell them, "You've shown me this one already," backed up by, "I have a good memory for faces you know."

She studied each photo, "I know so many people, but none of these."

"Do you know any Jews?" asked the one with the lisp.

"No."

She thought of that day in June, outside the park, she had met Ellen who was out shopping; several people had glanced their way. Ellen's clothes were well-worn whereas hers were brand-new, they were standing next to the '*Kein Entritt für Juden*', (Entry for Jews is forbidden) at the park entrance.

The other said, "You do know what happens to people consorting with Jews, aiding them, offering them shelter, hiding valuables for them."

The lisper told her as he stared at her, "You will end up in a work camp for several years. There you will learn to mend your ways."

"I have no Jewish friends," she replied pleasantly.

In one case, when asked if she had she ever been to such and such a place, she had answered, "I may have gone there with my parents."

They asked if she had overheard a quietly spoken conversation, a mention of the German Communist or Socialist party, any dissident talk concerning the Fuhrer or other party members. She kept her answers short the whole time, answering softly with a polite, "No."

She knew they had, in their eyes, the right to question her, but they were only fishing. They had no evidence of her affiliation to the Communist party; she had used her literary skills to write about the Nazis, typing propaganda for the illegal press, numerous flysheets. She had passed these on many times in different ways to one of a dozen people she knew only by face. The only evidence to her affiliation to the German Communist Party had now disappeared; all she had to do was sit tight, wish for the best, hoping nobody had seen her brother running off with her typewriter.

The darkness startled her as the light extinguished, then a bare, low-watt bulb did its best to illuminate the room once more; as her eyes adjusted to the dimness, she could make out her antagonists.

They stood at the doorway, regarding her.

She stared back, looking from one to the other. One of them had questioned her at home, but the other was a stranger. He was the one with the effeminate voice. He had a Hitler Schnautze, a toothbrush moustache, favoured by that pontificating, bombastic loudmouth, who most people, for obvious reasons, admired.

He now stood there with his overcoat draped over his shoulders like a cape, despite the heat from the radiator in the small stuffy room, looking down his nose at her. Then he half-turned his head, looked sideways to his companion who opened the door, left without a word, leaving the Hitler impersonator standing there. He gave Elfriede his impression of a threatening glare then left the room, slamming the door behind him.

Elfriede stifled a nervous laugh, wondering what was going to happen next.

Conclusion.

After first knocking, he entered the room, the interior lit by a lamp on the other's desk. Appearing somewhat sheepish, he said, "I think someone is arsing us about sir, something that should not be taken lightly by us of the Gestapo." He ran his fingers through his hair, paced back and forth, fingering his moustache.

He glanced at his superior, seated behind his desk, he knew his boss resented his family's high position in society; he looked forward to the day when he was in charge of Hamburg Gestapo.

The older man, an ex-police officer, eyed the other with concealed disdain, *'What does he look like with that stupid moustache, the damn pansy? Gestapo my arse, he only got this job because of his uncle's high status within the Nazi party and it was his informant that led us to this so-called communist suspect.'*

Leaning forward, he asked him quietly, "Why?"

The other man stopped pacing, struck a pose. Standing there, he took out his cigarette case and lighter; he extracted and lit a cigarette. "Well sir, it's like this, her family, Mollenhauer, they are well known athletes. They are Germany's heroes so to speak. Her sister took bronze at the Olympics, why I believe the Fuhrer presented her with the medal himself. Not only that, her brother was the first German radio sports reporter to give a live broadcast, did you know he even commented on the Olympics."

He lowered his voice, "I spoke to my father a few minutes

ago on the telephone, and he told me her family is sympathetic to the Fuhrer, he said somebody may have it in for her, you know how spiteful some people can be, and you know her brother is a member of the SS."

He sat back in his chair, he didn't give a shit what this idiot's father said, but he had to admit it, he had questioned hundreds of suspects, he knew when people were lying, especially with their voice high-pitched in denial, the quick glances to the left as they searched for an excuse or lied to them.

He had to face it; somebody had been leading them on and this woman's family would kick up a fuss if they arrested her on some trumped-up charge and God knows what connections her brother had in the SS. He did not want to find himself interviewing Russian prisoners thousands of miles away in the arctic wastes just because of this prattling baboon, posing in front of him like that spaghetti, Mussolini.

He had already written out a full report, putting his subordinate in a very bad light, but told him, "She may have, unwittingly, had contact with these communists. She said she entertained a lot, and we know how these people move around, finding it safer in a crowd. It is probably a misunderstanding on somebody's part, so you will now apologize nicely to Fraulein Mollenhauer on my behalf and escort her back to her apartment."

"Do you think it a good idea to keep an eye on her place, you never know, her commie guests may unwittingly return, without her knowledge I mean?"

One look from his superior was enough. He stepped back, stood to attention, raised his arm stiffly saying, "Heil Hitler."

The man at the desk repeated the phrase quietly, raised his hand as if in dismissal, watching as the other left his office.

Chapter four.

Classification.

Hamburg, October 1938.

He pushed open the door and entered the room, and forcing a smile he called out, "I er, er, received notification to report here today," and glanced at his wristwatch. "My n-name is Johannes Kaempfer I, er, I'm not late am I?"

"Sit!"

He dropped the grimace, closed the door quickly and glanced around the room: a spartan affair, adorned with Hitler portraits and propaganda posters. A plain wooden chair stood in front of a large wooden desk, he hurried over to it. He stopped and his jaw dropped, he raised his right arm and said, "Heil Hitler", and on seeing that the other did not intend to reply, he sat down.

The man in the yellow khaki uniform, sitting behind his desk stared at him. His armband displayed the Nazi symbol, a swastika, he wore the Nazi party badge on his uniform lapel. He said, "Herr Kaempfer, you are aware of the new legislation are you not? The letter I sent you was for your own good."

Kaempfer felt the other's eyes boring into his; he lowered his gaze, nodding rapidly. "Yes, sir, I am, sir."

"Unless you decide otherwise, you are to receive new papers; you will be re-classified as from today."

"Re-classified, sir, I, er, I don't understand!"

"You just told me you were aware of the new legislation, you are married to a Jewess, so you will be, unfortunately, re-classified as a Jew." He sneered, saying, "That is to say, a half-Jew."

"B-but I am only - as you said - married to one."

The sneer turned to an expression of disgust. "You have had sexual intercourse with her, have you not? Despoiling the Aryan pureness"

"But, sir, she is my wife."

"Then divorce her," he said, somewhat louder, glaring at him.

Kaempfer said, "How, sir, on what grounds?"

"In my opinion, you have the legal right to divorce her because she is Jewish. Under the new legislation, that alone will be reason enough." He pushed a form across to him. "Just fill in this form and sign it, then you can keep your original pass and that will be the end of it. But remember, Herr Kaempfer, you can no longer live together."

Kaempfer had heard rumours, deportation, work camps for undesirables and the like and he realised he could be implicated, lose his job. He rose and approached the desk, the official handed him a fountain pen. "Their days are numbered anyway, these Jews, these pariahs," he added, "And you will thank the Fuhrer for this, one day."

Kaempfer took the pen, leaned forward, peering at the form. He noted the reference to German citizens married to Jewish, half-Jewish, and other non-Aryan races, a paragraph about 'Rassenschande' pertaining to keeping the purity of the Aryan race. He looked at the official. Before he could speak, the other said, "You are going to sign it aren't you? You do understand the implications, the problems facing you married to a Jew."

Kaempfer nodded. "Yes, yes, I was..." the man's glare terrified him, so cold, empty, and callous. He looked down at the form once again, quickly filled it in, his hands shaking. He finished by signing it, then straightened up, handing back the pen.

The other took it beaming, his eyes soft, his tone now warm, friendly, "Now that wasn't difficult, was it?"

Kaempfer stood there in silence.

The other said with a half-smile, "What do they call you, your friends; Hanness is it?"

Kaempfer nodded.

"You may leave now, Hanness, thank you, you were very helpful," said the other.

Kaempfer turned and walked towards the door in a daze.

The man called out, "Er, Hanness, please be so kind as to send your, er, ex-wife in," adding, with a raised arm as Kaempfer turned to him, "Heil Hitler."

Kaempfer responded half-heartedly, then he opened the door, left the room.

He closed the door, walked towards a slim, dark-haired woman in her mid-forties, his wife, Ellen. She sat on one of the wooden chairs in the narrow hallway, next to another woman.

He looked down at her, her face still held traces of her youthful beauty. Their time together flashed through his mind; all the way back to their wedding day - in this very same building, years ago. He remembered the Christmases, the birthdays, not forgetting the disappointment when the doctor told him he was sterile, Ellen's face when he told her. He took a deep breath, let it out slowly, saying quietly, "You can go in now."

Ellen Kaempfer rose up. "What's happened, Hanness', you look awful?"

"I, I , I'm alright, it's just-." He looked at her. She gazed back, her soft brown eyes wide. He felt defeated and said, "He's waiting."

She examined his features, and then she walked towards the office door.

As the door closed, Kaempfer looked down at Ellen's older sister, Betty. The two women had received a letter similar to his, delivered by a police officer on the same day. She stared back at him. "What took you so long in there, what did they want?"

He tried to speak, but his throat ached, he felt the tears coming. He rushed off down the hallway, wiping his face, wishing he were far, far away from this dreadful place.

***

Ellen knocked and entered the room; she raised her right arm, said quietly, "Heil Hitler."

The man behind the desk stared at her and held out his hand. "Your pass."

She took her pass out of her handbag, stepped forward, handed it over. He snatched it, opened it up, took a stamp, pressed it onto the page. He picked up a pen scribbled something, then handed the pass back.

She examined the page, he'd added the name "Sarah" to her forenames, he'd also stamped a large letter 'J' below her photo, her marital status now stood at Divorced.

"Excuse me, there seems to be some mistake, my first name is Ellen, but you have added 'Sarah' and I'm not divorced."

The man actually beamed as he told her, "All Jewesses are to carry the name "Sarah" in their pass, as for your marital status, you are divorced, your husband signed the application form just five minutes ago after taking my advice."

Her heart stood still, her breath caught in her throat. "W- w – why did -?"

"Had he not, he could have been classified as a Jew."

"But he and I never spoke of divorce, we didn't-."

"I have no time to discuss this, get out of my office, now."

***

Outside on the street, Kaempfer breathed in the cold air, his body shaking. He slowly came to a decision, mumbling to himself, "I'd better go home and pack, yes, yes, an – and then afterwards to the bank." He panted heavily as he hurried along. "And I - I can stay with my cousin for the time be -." He stopped, his visage crumpled, he clutched his chest, as he gasped for breath the thought came, '*God is punishing me*'.

Delayed shock had caused his heart muscle to rupture slightly, but painfully, followed by the realisation at what he had done to his wife, their way of life. He burst into tears, sobbing uncontrollably, unaware of the stares from the passers-by.

***

Ellen came out of the office, her face white. Betty, ten years her senior, stood up, went to her, held her close. "Whatever is the matter?"

"He, he has - divorced me, Haenes' has divorced me - so as not to be classed as a Jew, he - he didn't even ha - ha - have to discuss it with me." She sobbed quietly, then said as her sister held her, "We may never see each other - ever again."

Betty stood there open-mouthed.

They both jumped as a loud voice called out, "Betty Holstein!"

***

The next day, post arrived for Ellen and Betty. Ellen looked at the logo on the envelope "Coutinho Cara & Co." Betty tore hers open, she took out the letter, read it through. "I thought so, we've been sacked."

Ellen looked at her letter; read it aloud, "Dear Mrs Kaempfer, due to circumstances beyond our control, we must sadly inform you that your services are no longer required."

Betty screwed the paper up, retorted, "That's what I said, we've been sacked."

Chapter five.

Hamburg, Luneberger Heide.

Hans.

Elfriede looked at the scenery, the Luneberger Heide, south of Hamburg. The countryside seemed to go on forever, with its wooded hills, flowing river. It was nature's paradise, a sight to be in awe of at any time of year.

In five months time, in August, the heath would be a blaze of colour, pink-lilac and white from the heather blooms. She breathed in deeply, exalting in the scented air, she felt the weight lift from her tired shoulders, she felt alive once more.

She just had to get away from the city for a while. She felt ashamed, disgusted at the sight of those swaggering brown-shirted bullies, roaming the city streets displaying their black, red, and white swastika armbands. She thought of Ellen and their chance meeting a few months ago. The rumours about work camps for non-Aryans.

She'd heard nothing positive from her controller about passes or travel documents for Ellen and her sister On the one occasion she'd passed him in the street, outside the coffee shop, their old meeting place, over a month ago, he'd walked on without any sign of recognition, ignoring her presence completely. She felt desolate, for all she knew, he could be in prison or even dead.

She knew she dared not turn to her family for help, for being Evangelists; they were also pro-Nazi, something that had turned her away from the church.

She walked on, along the pathway, amongst the trees; she wandered by a stream, putting thoughts of city life out of her head, listening to the humming of the insects.

A blackbird called out a warning, "Kik - kik - kik - kik," as it flew across her path, glided, chattering, into the foliage.

On hearing a noise behind her, she stopped, turned around. There she saw a man about her age as he approached her. He was dressed like her, for hiking, knee-length trousers, woollen socks, sturdy leather boots, a tweed jacket, and a bright yellow pullover over an open-necked white shirt. He was carrying a small rucksack on his back.

He smiled as he approached her. "Good morning, a beautiful day is it not?"

She smiled, regarded his pose; dark hair combed back from a

strong brow. His stance was neither dominating nor subservient and his smile was something else. A tickling sensation ran down her spine, a strange feeling, the opposite of foreboding, filling her senses. "Good morning, yes it is rather nice here, in fact nice is not a good enough word, even the word beautiful does not do it justice."

He stopped a few metres away, and they stood gazing at one another for a short eternity, neither one the least bit uncomfortable, then he took a step forward. "Allow me to introduce myself; my name is Thunsdorff, Hans Thunsdorff."

He offered her his hand, she took it, noticing the absence of a wedding ring. "Pleased to meet you, Mr Thunsdorff, my name is Elfriede Mollenhauer, I live in Hamburg, I have an apartment there."

He released her hand, he'd seen the minute glance at his hand and knew what she'd sought. "The pleasure is all mine," he said, "I was born in Kiel but I work in Berlin, I have my own apartment there and I have never seen Hamburg City, they tell me it is quite nice."

His voice had a pleasant tone, warm, friendly, inviting, she replied in kind saying, "It is, and I have never been to Berlin, is it nice there too?"

He pulled a face and shrugged lightly, then smiled at her questioning expression. "In a way I suppose, it's a big and beautiful city, full of people rushing around," he added, "What is your occupation?"

Her frown vanished as she said,"I'm a secretary, what is yours?"

"I am a mathematician; I work for a large insurance firm in Berlin."

For some unknown reason she told him. "Norway is nice in summer. I was planning to take a trip there one day, to visit the cities and journey through the Fjords," which was of course true, but she hadn't finalised any plan at the moment.

He looked at her, his eyes still smiling, "I am staying at the Waldrodeln Inn in the village, I booked in this morning, Do you know it?"

A thought flashed through her mind. '*Is this Kismet, Schicksal, fate that has brought us together,*' She said quickly, "Yes, I'm staying there too, but I'm leaving tomorrow, unfortunately."

His face fell slightly as he said quietly, "Yes, unfortunately, is the right word."

Her heart skipped a whole beat at his reply and she added enthusiastically, "But I will be visiting friends in Berlin this summer." Something she had been intending to do for a while.

At the sound of her animated outburst, he brightened up visibly. "And I always wanted to tour Hamburg."

She ran her eyes over him, his stature, his warm smile. *'He is rather forward, but charming, and he is not one bit arrogant and overbearing; what a change.'*

"Would you accept my invitation to lunch, Miss Mollenhauer?"

Her heart fluttered, *'Why not!'* and she heard herself say, "Thank you, I accept."

"Shall we say twelve noon? I have reserved a table."

"Twelve noon it is," she said, her whole being tingling.

He looked around him. "Well, I'm new here; would you care to show me around?"

She stretched out her hand saying, "Gladly." Smiling as he took it.

Hamburg docks.

The passenger ship, Gorge, docked at Hamburg on her return from Norway, adding a dash of colour to her surroundings as she passed her grey-painted sisters, cold, silent ships of war.

Elfriede and Hans, together now for just over a year, left the ship after their weeklong holiday, spent sailing along the Fjords, sleeping in separate cabins, and visiting the small towns and villages along the coast.

On their departure, Christian, one of the stewards, a Dane, told them when they were alone, "I am afraid this will be the Gorge's last journey for a while for some, er, unknown reason."

Elfriede said, "Oh dear, we were looking forward to next year or maybe sooner."

Hans said nothing, his features changing only when he handed Christian his "trinkgelt" for the journey, after which he bowed and thanked them politely and left with their baggage.

Once on deck, they collected their luggage and left the ship. On the quay, Elfriede looked at the smartly-painted vessel, their transport through the Norwegian fjords. She and Hans had found the Norwegians polite and hospitable, but sensed rather than saw a certain apprehension when spoken to in Norwegian with a German accent.

She looked along the quay lined with ships of war and several cargo ships, grubby in comparison with the Gorge, and at the large numbers of soldiers assembled there. She turned to the distant noise with Hans and saw military vehicles, tanks, and artillery as they trundled noisily along the roadways between the buildings. She gazed around her frowning, she, Hans and the passengers from the Gorge, were the only civilians there, she asked quietly. "What is going on?"

He glanced around him and keeping his voice low, he told her, "Invasion."

She looked at him in fear. "Invasion!" she said, copying his tone, "Where, Denmark?"

He nodded and whispered, "Yes, in the near future and Norway too, Hitler wants control of the whole of Europe. Somebody quoted him as saying, 'Today Germany, tomorrow the world'."

She looked at him aghast, "You can't be serious?"

He looked at her, "We are facing war, my dear, war in Europe, I am certain Hitler will order the invasion of Poland, and I believe he will dupe the Russians into helping him. Then Russia will be the next step. I believe Hitler will seek peace with Britain. Italy and France will compromise somehow, and then the road to Africa will be open, and do not forget Fascist Spain. Hitler's only foreseeable problem is oil, fuel for his war machine. I imagine he has his eye on the Balkans too, his problem there is Mussolini."

She looked at him in earnest saying what was foremost in her mind. "What about you?"

He said, "I have been approached by certain people in the military, I have been offered an officer's rank, a major, or something, but I will be damned before I join this madness as a soldier, they can take me as I am."

They turned as a voice over the tannoy system called out, "All civilians clear the quay area immediately."

Moving quickly to avoid the squads of soldiers and sailors, marching along the quay, they hurried along, walked through customs, after which they stood in line waiting for a taxi.

She said, "Let us forget about war for the time being, you are now to meet my family and they know everything about you," then she added, "Well almost everything."

He smiled, lifted up her hand, "And we can tell them the good news, also show off your engagement ring"

Hamburg City.

Autumn arrived, her twin brother, Robert, now a soldier home on leave, looked at her in surprise after embracing her. "You're marrying Hans this year?"

Elfriede grinned, nodded. She looked him over, he was even more handsome in his army uniform, his face lightly tanned, his hair shorn in the military style. "On September the seventh, Peter will be best man," she said.

His face fell, "Peter has been defined as a Jew hasn't he?"

She turned her face from him, led him to the sofa in her apartment lounge. They sat down together.

He raised his voice, startling her, "These people, these damn Nazi's, how dare they do such a thing, calling Peter a Jew as if it was a crime to be one."

"I know, Robert, it is awful, he has been classed as a half-Jew, as his mother is a Jewess, and he's joining the Army to prove his allegiance to the country he was born in." Then she smiled.

"Mother and Father have approved, Hans is well known in Berlin, and he is a highly qualified mathematician."

He looked at her questioningly, "It's a bit sudden isn't it?"

She smiled at him, then she said, "Dear, Robert, it's not what you think, Hans, and I have known each other for a while now and we are well suited, we have a lot in common, we are fond of each other and at times like these one has to have someone to come home to."

He nodded saying, "I saw those two women the other day, the ones we were talking with in the park that summer, one of them, the younger, Ellen I think, wanted to know how you were; said I was to give you their regards."

Her face saddened, she nodded, wondering if he knew. "They are Jewish you know."

He replied, "I know that, what I don't understand is why they are still here, it's silly of them to stay really, they could be deported to a work camp."

She told him, "They aren't rich Jews, Robert, and they know no-one outside of Hamburg, let alone France or England. Anyway Betty, the oldest, is too old to travel; she suffers terribly from arthritis and lumbago." She shook her head, "It doesn't seem fair somehow, there's no reason to force them to leave the country they were born in. They are German just like you and me."

He nodded, "I agree, life is unfair, and I've heard they are sending foreigners to work in factories here in Hamburg, forced labour they called it."

Her face coloured, her voice rose, "Whatever for, they aren't criminals."

He edged closer and placed an arm around her; he pulled her gently to him, "You tried once to arrange safe passage for them didn't you, through your, er, friend?"

She shook her head, "It is best that you forget about that part of my life for your own good." She added, "I would help them if I could, but I don't know how, I feel so helpless."

He said, "My brave sister, still fighting for a lost cause."

"I'm not the only one; fascism is not confined to Germany, look at Italy, France, and that stupid man in England, Mosley and his Blackshirts, even some members of the Deutsche-Amerikan Bund in the USA are siding with the Nazis, and don't forget Spain."

He sighed, "Yes, you lost friends there in the fighting didn't you."

She said, "You did too, if the truth were known, and don't forget the bombings." She added, "You have read about the bombings, Guernica, the dead children, laid out in the streets?"

"Yes, sadly, I have, that's another reason to detest fascism."

She looked at him, silence reigned for a while, then she said, "Have you heard from our little brother Hans lately?"

"No, and I know why he doesn't write, he knows we hate the Nazis and all that they stand for."

She told him adamantly, "I haven't got time for hate, Robert. Hate is a waste of time, and after all is said and done, Hans is our brother and he is old enough to make up his own mind. I don't hate him because he joined the SS; I love him just as much as I love you and the others, despite the current situation." She turned in her seat, faced him bodily, and said softly, "You take care out there, look after yourself, please, dear brother."

He smiled. "Don't you worry; this whole thing will be over soon after it has started."

She wondered if he knew something she didn't or if it was all wishful thinking on his part.

Chapter six.

1941.

The package.

Outside, Ellen looked up at the almost cloudless sky. The streets of Hamburg were quieter now with most of the male population gone to the armed forces. She had heard people saying proudly that Europe belonged to the Third Reich, and the announcement on the radio about the British being stupidly defiant, even after most of their aircraft and airfields had been destroyed in a courageous attack by the German air force, during which the British air force had the audacity to bomb Berlin, causing Adolf Hitler to promise devastation in retaliation.

When Hitler came to power, she had rejoiced with most other people. She saw Hitler as her country's saviour; but the people who worked for him were only too eager to abuse the power given to them. The police were powerless to stop the brown-shirted hooligans; her non-Jewish neighbours told her they were only voicing their own opinions, as was their right.

Forced to walk in the gutter because she was Jewish, she passed people in the street, some of them, on seeing the Star of David on her coat, pretended not to notice her, others appeared embarrassed, several couples even looked at her in sadness. She looked at a young couple as they passed her, a young woman on the arm of a soldier on leave, both of them oblivious of the world around them.

Then she saw '*them*' approaching, three of them, using the whole pavement, strutting along in step. She walked on, keeping her head down. She heard the remark, "Well that's one Jewish whore who knows her place."

Then his comrade's jocular reply, "There won't be any left soon."

She stopped, gasped, "The work camps." Then she made her way home, her shopping trip forgotten.

Back once more in their apartment, she thought of the things she wanted to take with her, as it seemed to her that her and Betty's departure could be any day now.

"Betty, we have to pack for our journey."

Betty picked up a small suitcase, "I did mine while you were out, toiletries, a blouse, a skirt, stockings and all my underwear; I couldn't fit anything more inside."

Ellen sorted out her things; packed the essentials, spare clothing, mainly underclothing, in a small suitcase along with toiletries, soap and a large hand towel. Then she thought about the things left over, amongst them were things she valued most and she had no desire to lose them. Maybe she could make a parcel up, leave it at the post office. Then she remembered Jews weren't allowed to use the postal service any more. She thought about what she should do with such a parcel, but she had no idea. She thought about it for a short while then decided she would ask her friend Elfriede what to do with it. She knew there were severe penalties for people helping Jews to hide their valued possessions, but Elfriede seemed to her to be a capable, level-headed person; she would advise her what to do in any case.

She went through her belongings once more and sorted out what she treasured most. Maybe Elfriede could keep her things until they returned when this silly war was over. With this plan in mind, she picked up her photo album and went through the photos, she looked at one in particular, trying to remember when she had it taken, somewhere out in the countryside with friends from their schooldays. Her hair was longer then, she was wearing a light beige outfit. She smiled at the memory of that day, a day with friends, friends who were long gone, some to England, some to America, she wished now that she and Betty had gone with them.

She placed the album with the rest of her things laid out on the table and packed them in an embroidered table cover. She took a sheet of used packing paper, made a parcel of her things, tying it up with string.

Betty, slicing bread for their evening meal, said, "What are you going to do with that parcel?"

"I'm giving it to Elfriede for safe keeping; she can keep it safe for when we return."

"Do you really think your loud-mouthed friend Adolf will use two old women like us?"

Ellen's brow creased. "I wish you wouldn't call him that, he is not my friend. Anyway
Germany needs people like us for the war effort, they will need office workers, and we are fully qualified."

Betty snorted, "Qualified! We are unemployable because we are Jewish; we were sacked, thrown out onto the street and dear sister, we are running short of cash, which is why we live together now."

Ellen looked at her sister saying softly, "Our employer was forced to relieve us of our positions, it's the law now, unfair I know, but he, like many others, had no choice, and my friend Adolf as you call him, did not make all these laws, he has more important things to do, we are at war you know."

"I know that, Betty. It took your Wilhelm away from you, he hasn't written for a while, has he?"

"He could be dead for all I know."

"You mean he broke off your relationship?"

One look at Betty's expression was enough to know that her boyfriend had stopped writing because Betty was a Jewess. She sniffed. "Anyway, a fine husband your Herr Kaempfer turned out to be, divorcing you so as not to be classified as a Jew."

Ellen remained silent, the memory of betrayal too painful for comment.

Hamburg. September 1941.

They turned the corner. "This is it, Bert, Eichenstrasse."

Norbert Reiterhaus, police officer, walked through the drizzle with his colleague. They faltered in mid-stride, he swore, "Shit – bloody hell!" and lashed out with his foot at a black cat, moving stealthily across their path. The cat, a large beast, turned on him, hissing, baring its teeth. He spat at it, asked as it ran off. "What's the house number, Max?"

Max, just turned nineteen, looked down at his wet clipboard, and said, "Number 22." He was happy with his work, his father was a police inspector; both his uncles were high-ranking police officers. Max was also a proud member of the Nazi party, a staunch supporter of Hitler, just like his father and his uncles, a good enough reason for not joining the Wermacht and getting yourself killed.

Norbert grunted and asked, "How many?"

Max answered tiredly, "Two of them, female, Betty Holstein and Ellen Kaempfer, apartment eleven."

Norbert looked at the numbers as they walked along the

street and found the right one. He pushed the door open, it squeaked on its hinges, he stepped inside. He scratched at the long scar on his jaw line, received during a bar-brawl and it always itched when he was irritated.

Max said, "First floor, and top of the stairs, both of them on the left."

Norbert led the way up the stairs found the apartment. He banged with his fist on the door, shouted, "Schutzpolizei, open up."

They waited a few seconds then the door opened. A frightened face appeared and asked fearfully, "Whatever is the matter, what has happened?" causing Max to snigger.

The other ignored her question, not hiding his accumulated distaste for Jews as he said with his lip curled back, "What's your name?"

The woman, wearing an apron, brushed back a strand of hair from her face. "Ellen Kaempfer, I live here."

He turned to Max who nodded; he looked at the list and asked her, "Where's Betty Holstein, is she here?"

A voice sounded within the apartment, "I am here, what do you want?"

Ellen stepped back quickly, opening the door wider so they could see the other woman, leaning forward, supporting herself on the back of a leather sofa.

Norbert thrust a scrap of paper in the first woman's hands, said, "As of tomorrow, all Jews over six years of age are to wear the Star of David on the front and back of their outer clothing, visible to all, if you fail to do so you will be severely punished, that's the address where you can purchase your emblems." With that, he turned on his heel and strode off.

Ellen heard him ask the other, "Where to now?"

"Another apartment, third floor, twenty blocks away," was the answer.

"And how many more, before lunch-time?"

"Three!"

"Shit!"

Ellen closed the door, looked at the piece of paper. She knew the address, one of the local tailors. The shop, boarded up earlier was now open, she recalled seeing one morning the brown-shirts quietly removing the planking, ushering an elderly couple inside.

Betty asked, "Is the meal ready, I'm starving?"

Ellen told her, "Yes, it's ready, go and sit down, I'll set the table."

Jude.

Ellen looked at her sister Betty as she limped by her on her way to the bathroom, she said, "How's your back, dear, any better?"

Betty answered in her usual way, "It keeps on reminding me that I am human and still alive."

"How are your knees, I saw you limping this morning?"

"My knees are fine," she lied, "they haven't troubled me for a long time."

Betty recalled the last visit to her doctor who had left Hamburg after *'The night of the Long Knives'* when Synagogues were desecrated, burned. A number of Jewish money-lenders were brutally murdered, robbed by drunken hooligans. He'd told her, *'You have arthritis in both of your knees. I suggest you move to warmer climes, Spain or Italy, the air would be better for your sister too, as her bronchitis was worse last winter.'*

"Spain, Italy!" her sister had said, "That would be nice."

She'd said, "Maybe we can buy a hacienda or a villa on the coast. How do you think we should travel, by limousine or train?" Then she added, "I should live so long, Ellen. We can hardly afford to eat properly, if it wasn't for our late downstairs neighbour, we would have starved by now."

Ellen recalled old Mrs Dorn, a cripple, who she went shopping for. She always ordered too much and when she gave Ellen and Betty any groceries she would say, *'I have found I have too much flour'* or *'The doctor says I eat too much sugar'* and *'I cannot eat a whole cabbage or loaf and it is a shame to throw it away.'* The old woman had passed on last year on New Years day, at the age of ninety-two. They were the only ones at her funeral and were surprised to find out she had mentioned them in her will to the tune of two thousand Reichmarks, an amount handed to them by the priest. These funds were now dwindling away.

Ellen put down the wooden sewing box, a birthday present from her husband of years ago. She threaded a needle, picked up the last Star of David, a piece of bright yellow cloth with the word *'Jude'* printed on it. The weather had turned cold, winter was drawing nearer. She took hold of her sister's overcoat, started to sew in small neat stitches.

Sitting on the sofa, she looked at the emblem, the Star of David. The Israelite warriors wore this on their shields eons ago, to show their enemy who they were facing, and thinking of that, she felt proud of her heritage, proud to be Jewish. She and her sister were a long way from Palestine, but that did not matter, for her homeland was Germany.

They were well aware of the humiliation the Jews of Hamburg were suffering daily, they had seen the beatings, had suffered degradation. They had seen the men in brown shirts, the swastika badges, distributing leaflets to the public, they had seen the Star of David daubed on the shop windows of Jewish establishments, the ones that weren't broken that is.

All of her Jewish friends had departed one by one; they had left the country with their families and she remembered a conversation with a close non-Jewish friend, a number of years ago, just as these troubles began. *'Come with us, Wilfried has a brother in America; he can obtain visas for the pair of you, it will be easy as your husband isn't Jewish.'*

She hadn't accepted, as she couldn't leave Betty who was

very ill at the time with influenza and bronchitis. She had thought of what her husband would have done, he probably would have jumped at the chance, but he had divorced her anyway not wanting to be classed as a half-Jew.

Her neighbours shunned her and her sister as if they were lepers, afraid of the slur, *'Jewish sympathizers'*, all except one that is, her young friend Elfriede Mollenhauer. She and Betty had met Elfriede with her twin brother Robert, outside the park last week and she had told them everything, how she had married while in Berlin, but still had the same apartment in Hamburg, as her husband worked for the military in the capital.

She recalled her Jewish friend's tales of atrocities, of beatings, and of robberies in other cities. Serious doubt had formed in her mind as they told her stories of rich Jewish families, forced to sell their goods, jewellery, paintings and property for a mere pittance.

Today, this earlier doubt was fading rapidly. She had not been sure whether the talk about work camps for the Jews where they would work 'for the glory of the Third Reich', was true or not, until the police officer cheerfully informed her.

Whatever it was, she hoped that if chosen, it would be for a secure secretarial position, and she wondered what she and her sister should take with her and what should they leave behind. She had heard that deportees, as these workers were named, Jews, like her and Betty, had left with very little luggage, after which the brown-shirted 'Meshugge', Rudolf Hess's bullies, as some people called them in private, plundered their houses and property, and she wondered what she should do before the police came for her and her sister. She finished sewing the Star of David on her sister's overcoat, remembering the police officer's threats after he brought them.

Nowadays, as a Jew, you kept your mouth shut, walked in the gutter. If the brown-shirted thugs spotted a man or a woman wearing a yellow star walking on the pavement, the result would be a severe beating. She looked at the clock, 11.15, she could do some shopping before the shops shut. She pulled on her overcoat saying, "I'm off shopping, Betty, but I will be home within the hour."

"Watch out you don't bump into your friend Adolf's pet dogs."

"He's not my friend, not any more," she answered.

Chapter seven.

Hamburg, March 13th 1941.

The bombing.

Elfriede finished ironing her husband's shirt as he shaved in the bathroom. He was on leave for a short while from duty in Berlin, where he was part of the Wehrmacht. He had stipulated, as he said he would, that he would not wear a uniform and had refused promotion, remaining a private, as he had no desire to be a soldier or an officer.

He had told her the other weekend, 'The party members resented me, calling me disloyal to my face, but I do my job well, better than anyone else can do it, and as the Army needs my services desperately as a code breaker, they relented.'

At that moment the door buzzer sounded. She walked over to the door, opened it. There stood Ellen Kaempfer, her Jewish friend, smiling widely, her long dark hair fashioned in a neat bun; she held a paper package in both hands. "Good evening, Elfriede, how are you, it's been a long time?"

Elfriede said, "Good evening, Ellen, nice to see you again, what can I do for you?" She stepped back and asked her, "Won't you come in for a while?"

Ellen said, "Thank you, no, I am sorry for the disturbance, but I won't keep you long. As you may know, Betty and me could be deported, we do not know when or where to. I have made a parcel of the things I can't take with me. I know it is forbidden but would you take care of them for me until me and Betty return, it might be a while though?"

Elfriede knew of the deportation orders, but she was still shocked to hear it from Ellen herself. She forced a smile, she nodded. "Of course I'll take care of your things. Promise to write to me as soon as you arrive at your place of work. Hans and I haven't decided whether to stay here or not, but I will see to it that our mail is forwarded. So, tell me, how is Betty?"

She said, "Getting old, like me."

Elfriede gazed at the tired-looking woman with the yellow Star of David on her coat. Her heart went out to her, those damn Nazi bastards, their deportation orders. All Jews must be prepared to move at a moment's notice; they would be told they were being transported to some place where they would work for the glory of the fatherland. Some people; especially employers, had spoken out against it and had received a severe beating for their pains.

She held out her hands, Ellen handed the paper package to her; she took it, lost for words. She had tried to obtain visas for them, but without success, it seemed the suspicions voiced at that time by a friend were now coming true.

She could not help Ellen or her sister now, other countries had closed their borders to Jews years ago, the chance of escape was gone. She looked at her; she had lost weight. "Are you sure you won't you come in for a while?"

Ellen smiled, shook her head. "I'd rather not, it is getting late, and I don't want to get you involved."

"We should care what people say or think."

Ellen said, "I must go now, Elfriede, Betty is waiting for me, and they could come any time now." She smiled bravely and with a little wave, said, "To our next meeting."

As she turned to go, Elfriede put on her best smile, holding the package to her breast. "I will take care of it, Ellen, until you return that I promise and we will see each other again. When you come back, we will have a big party," she added, "I hope it's nice where you are going and if you can, please write to us, the sooner the better."

She closed the apartment door as Ellen walked off. She walked slowly back into the lounge, placed the package on the table next to her handbag. She saw Hans, as he came out of the bathroom. She turned away slightly, wiped away the tear as it rolled down her cheek.

He picked up his shirt, put it on, smiled at her as he buttoned it up. "It's still warm," he said, approached and kissed her on the lips. They embraced for a short while, he said, "I have to leave tomorrow afternoon. Won't you come with me?"

She was about to answer when they heard the air-raid sirens. Without another word, they picked up their street apparel, dressing quickly. Elfriede took the package and they left the apartment.

***

They heard the faint sound of anti-aircraft guns in the distance, the fainter sound of the ack-ack shells, as they ran to the shelter with others. Bright beams searched the darkening sky around them, Hans said, "They're early, they usually wait until it's totally dark."

Hans picked up a small boy who was struggling to keep up with his mother who was carrying his infant sister. The child looked at him in surprise, then smiled as Hans said, "Look, you can fly, you are a bird, an aeroplane," and swung the giggling boy round several times and then held on to him.

As they arrived at the shelter, he set the boy down inside the entrance. The woman turned to him. "Thank you, sir, these two are quite a handful; my husband is away, serving with the Navy."

Hans said, "It was a pleasure, I believe he enjoyed the flight."

Elfriede saw the sign in big letters over the shelter doorway. *'Jews forbidden',* and as they descended the stairway she thought of Ellen, where she was right now. She would be on her way home but she still had quite a way to go. She looked at the package, pressed to her side with her handbag, wondering when she would see her again.

They sat down with the others on a long bench in a narrow room, lit with several naked light bulbs. No sooner had the shelter door slammed shut when a tremendous explosion shook whole the room. Dust and plaster fell from the ceiling, the occupants cried out in fear, mothers comforted their children. The shelter occupants, mostly women, children, old men, huddled together in small family groups, some staring wide-eyed at one another as more bombs fell some way off.

Elfriede looked at Hans, pressed her body against him. He placed an arm around her shoulder, taking her hand in his other one saying, "Don't be afraid, I'm with you. Look at me, am I afraid?"

She smiled. "Probably, but you don't show it, you'd be a fool not to be, but you do give me strength."

A small child whimpered, baby cried out. It quietened down eventually as its mother sang a lullaby to it.

Elfriede winced, ducked like the others, including Hans, as a huge bomb exploded somewhere above them, showering them with plaster, dousing the lights. Several women screamed, the children started crying and shouting.

Hans called out, "Be quiet, be quiet, don't panic, the bomb has probably hit the electricity supply cable. Just close your eyes, then you'll feel better."

His advice worked, as the room grew quiet once more, then the terrible sounds above them continued, but despite all the noise, the young woman with the baby sang lullaby after lullaby, encouraging the children to join in, then the lights flickered back on again.

Aftermath.

The bombardment continued into the night; some people slept, some told the children fairy tales, others sang with them. Close to dawn, the bombing dissipated and after what seemed an age the all-clear sounded. An old man said, "Listen, it sounds like they've finished."

The children ceased their singing, and they listened.

The woman hugged her baby to her and said. "Yes, they've gone now."

Another voice, a female, said, "I bloody well hope so; I didn't have time to finish sorting out my washing."

They made their way up the stairs, pushed the door open despite the rubble, stumbling out into the morning light, shielding their eyes. The air was blue, smelled of wood smoke, an imitation fog, obliterating the surrounds. An elderly couple, the man, using his walking stick like a blind man's cane, led the way. He called out, "Damnation, I can't see a thing."

The woman, hanging on to him, said, "There's never much to

see after a bombing." The pair remained standing still on the pavement, afraid to move, listening with the others to the distant sounds of the fire engines.

Someone remarked, "Sounds like the stock yards were the target."

A breeze partially cleared the air, the people from the shelter gazed about them, some of them wishing they had remained blind as they gazed upon the new skyline.

"Oh my God, look at the smoke, they've hit the warehouses," said a man, pointing to billowing clouds of black smoke rising to the sky in the distance.

"And the goods yards," said his companion.

"Damned British," replied the other.

"It's the goods trains they're after," said another.

"Look at the buildings, the apartments, oh my God," said an elderly woman.

Where once had stood a complete row of apartment blocks there now was a huge, jagged gap in the middle, giving view to other damaged buildings beyond.

A middle-aged woman said, "Well I can forget about sorting

out my washing, my bloody apartment is gone, and three blocks with it." Her mouth fell open and she fell to her knees, calling out, "Mother of Christ," while crossing herself then she pointed through the shifting smoke from the burning apartment block ruins. Dozens of bodies lay smouldering, scattered amongst the rubble along the other side of the road. Men, women, children, battered and burnt, blown out of their apartments during the bombing.

"Why didn't they use the shelter," said somebody.

"They were on their way ere' an' got caught, some of em' probly' got hit by that big un' at the start," said an old crone.

Another woman gagged, said, "Oh, my God," indicating with her finger.

The crowd looked in the direction, saw a dead horse lying on the pavement over to their left, its entrails and bloody innards hanging out from its split belly. The cart it had pulled lay on its side; beyond it, the driver lay propped up against the wall as if taking a rest, his head hanging at an awkward angle.

"Oh, the poor horse," said a young mother, clutching her baby to her, "the poor man."

Somebody asked, "What was he doing out so late?"

"He was on his way home, he's a coalman," said the old man.

"Oh, God, look at her."

They turned as one, peering through the smoke, saw a girl, not more than sixteen years old, lying naked, close to the side of the road some twenty metres farther on to the right with her arms by her side, her legs stretched out, closed primly together. She appeared to be sleeping contentedly, as if unaware what had befallen her.

Elfriede approached her quickly, felt for a pulse while kneeling down in the dirt beside her. After finding none she looked at the left side of the girl's face and head, badly scorched. A woman gave her a bed sheet, ripped from someone's washing line by a bomb blast, to cover the corpse. She folded the girl's arms across the upper body, hiding the small breasts, and then gently laid the cotton sheet over her, mouthing a prayer as she tucked the edges beneath her fragile form.

Hans helped her to her feet; she dusted off her knees, looked up as a young police officer, aged about eighteen, came running up to them, hatless and out of breath. His uniform was torn and dirty, his hands were bleeding from several cuts. He skidded to a stop. His face, blackened with soot was streaked with tears, his hair, ginger, was singed in places. "There's a child trapped in a basement and I need help to get her out, so who's coming?"

Without a word, the crowd moved as one, hurriedly following the sobbing police officer. Elfriede said to Hans, "Poor fellow, so young too, when will this madness end?"

"I don't know," said Hans, "I just don't know," then he added in earnest, "Will you come with me tomorrow?"

She pulled him to her as they crossed the street, "Yes, I will come to Berlin with you; I may as well die there as anywhere else."

They hurried past buildings untouched by the bombing raid. They turned the last corner and stared more devastation. There stood the bare end of an apartment block, its windows blown out, with its remains smouldering.

A police officer lay in the centre of the road, unmoving. He had a vivid white scar leading from his chin all the way up to his ear. He stared at them with unseeing eyes as they passed.

They followed the young officer to the burnt-out shell seeing in the distance, ruined buildings dotting the shattered landscape, apartment blocks replaced by smoking rubble.

The young officer stopped, peeled off his uniform jacket.

"This is it," he cried, as he scrambled over the rubble, followed by Hans and the others. "I could hear her calling, I told her I would bring help, as some of the beams are too heavy for me."

***

After hours of toiling, assisted by other members of the public who emerged from their shelters, they extracted the child, a three-year-old girl, who called out to them continuously, miraculously unhurt. After continuing their search amongst the debris, they discovered nine older children hiding in a wine cellar, together with an elderly couple. They encountered numerous adult dead the little girl's parents included.

They laid the bodies in a row in the road, covering them with whatever material came to hand. Several of the women sobbed after recognising some of the dead. The young police officer called out as Elfriede and Hans left the scene, "I never thought it would come to this, it's not fair, all this bombing, damned bloody fascists."

Due to fallen buildings blocking the roads, Elfriede and Hans, tired, dirty, altered their journey back to her apartment. They walked down back alleys, along cobbled streets; they climbed over brick rubble, avoiding burst water pipes giving forth artificial rain.

Their complicated journey took them past a small, bombed-out building. A dozen elderly civilians busied themselves clearing the road of debris as if this were a normal every-day activity while others stood around, some dazed, some crying, consoled by others.

They looked at the building, minus the roof, a smouldering brick façade, displaying windows without glass, its shattered, blackened timbers smouldering quietly.

As they came to the corner, they saw several rows of what they thought were bundles of tattered rags, laid out in neat lines. As they came closer, they saw that the tiny bundles had small limbs with tiny fingers and toes, blackened hands and shoeless feet. The broken, burned bodies had bloodied faces, singed hair; some had their eyes closed as in slumber and others stared, frowning questioningly. Elfriede and Hans realized the building was a kindergarten.

Elfriede thought back to the children they had rescued from the bombed building, "Oh, God, dear God in heaven, I thought at first you spared children, have you then no pity at all?" She turned to Hans, aghast; he pulled her to his chest. He comforted her as she sobbed, watching as a small crowd of women rushed by, wailing terribly at the sight of the bodies, followed urgently by a priest and several nuns.

***

That evening they listened to the reports on the bombing raid. *'Last night the 13th of March, British bombers carried out a cowardly raid on Hamburg city's citizens, causing extensive damage, also causing the unwarranted deaths of fifty-one innocent men, women and children, including babies.'*

Elfriede dried her eyes, "Let's pack out things, I'm leaving with you."

Chapter Eight.

Deportation.

Hamburg. October 1941.

Ellen cleared away the breakfast dishes. She came out of the kitchen, heard someone knocking on the apartment door. She opened it, and there stood a police officer, old and sad-looking. "Ellen Kaempfer and Betty Holstein?"

Ellen, said, "Yes, that's right."

He squinted at his clip board, running his eyes across it, "You two are to report for deportation to the goods yards entrance at the main railway station on - the, - er, the day after tomorrow at, er, six o'clock sharp. You are allowed one suitcase. Don't be late."

With that, he walked away, his boots clumping on the wooden floorboards. Ellen closed the door. She saw Betty, staring at the closed door. "So, this is it. We're to be deported after all."

Ellen walked past her towards the bedroom, "We may as well eat all our food then."

***

The next day, Ellen looked at the calendar pinned to the kitchen cupboard, the 25th of October and then at the clock, eight thirty. She looked out of the window wondering about tomorrow.

She thought back to Elfriede on the day she brought her the package, recalled the terrifying journey home that evening in March, as the aircraft dropped their bombs, a raid that continued through the night and well into the small hours. She seemed to have had a guardian angel with her, as the bombs fell way behind her, landing on the buildings and on the main road she had run along just minutes before.

She had heaved a sigh of relief as she saw Eichenstrasse number 22, spared once more along with the other buildings and had wept with joy after finding Betty shivering with fear in their cellar.

She thought about Elfriede, hoped she was unharmed. She had received a letter from her saying she and her husband had moved to Berlin. She remembered how she had taken her package for safe keeping willingly, without hesitation, knowing the risk and although Elfriede had smiled at her, Ellen had still detected sadness in her eyes and behind the sadness something else, which she could not comprehend and hoped they would meet again, soon.

Now the package she had left with Elfriede became a package of hope, hope for their safe return, when this damn war was over.

She turned with a start to the hammering on her door, the hammering continued, then she realized it was her heart.

A voice screamed, "Open up; open up, Schutzpolizei, open up."

She called out as the hammering started once more, "I'm coming."

She opened the door and a man in black Gestapo uniform, holding a clipboard, barked out as he stepped between two police officers, "Ellen Kaempfer, Betty Holstein?"

Ellen nodded and said, "Yes, that's us."

He screamed, "Why weren't you at the station, you were told to report there?

Ellen stared at him. "We were told it was tomorrow, as you can see we have packed." She pointed to the two suitcases, quickly pulling on her overcoat, Betty copying her.

One of the police officers spoke up, "That will be Gunter, sir. He should have been pensioned off years ago, probably got the dates mixed up."

The Gestapo officer nodded, calmer now. "Yes, and now we will have round them all up ourselves."

Ellen picked up her and Betty's suitcase, the Gestapo officer nodded to the police officers. They grabbed hold of Ellen and Betty pulled them roughly into the corridor, hustled them out of the apartment block, onto the street.

Ellen looked at their transport, an old, canvas-covered army lorry, its wooden sides badly charred; she saw that she and Betty would not be the only passengers.

They struggled to climb aboard, willing hands from above aided them. As the tailboard slammed shut, they took a seat on one of the wooden benches. They looked at their fellow passengers, Jews like themselves, the Star of David visible on their clothing, half a dozen men and women who regarded them in silence.

The lorry made numerous stops along the way, loaded up adults and children of all ages, babies included. The SS soldiers and the Gestapo officer followed them in their Kubelwagen, only too eager to help the shocked, bewildered people with the aid of a kick or a shove towards the waiting vehicle.

On the long journey through the city, the lorry driver accelerated and braked harshly, oblivious to the needs of his passengers, not caring if they suffered injury or not, in fact it seemed that was his sole intention as they could hear him laughing.

The people standing, mostly men, having nothing to hang on to, jostled or fell against each other involuntarily. Several older people fell frequently to the boards, until they decided it was better to stay there.

The lorry drove through the city; passers-by looked up at them, some in despair, while others, dressed in their brown uniforms laughed and jeered, shouting. "Have a nice journey."

A seven-year-old girl passing by with her mother looked up at the rear of the lorry as it turned a corner, "Mummy, those people in that lorry, they have yellow stars on the clothes, what does that mean?"

The woman looked down at the child, forced a smile, "They are special people my dear, they have been chosen by our great leader to help the Fatherland in our struggle against oppression."

The child asked her, "Why weren't they smiling, why weren't they happy."

The woman sighed, "I don't know my dear; apparently some people don't know when they are better off."

She hurried on pulling the child with her, saying, "Uncle Gregor will be arriving home from Paris this afternoon; he says he has a lovely surprise for both of us."

***

After the last of the passengers were loaded, the Kubelwagen left them and the lorry driver tied up the canvas flap, sealing the occupants inside. Ellen and Betty sat with others in the semi-darkness. One of the passengers, peered through a small tear in the side canvas and remarked, "I think we're heading for the railway station."

A well-dressed woman holding on to her expensive-looking suitcase said, "I hope the carriages are clean, I've already laddered my stockings on this damn bench."

An old man turned to her. "Maybe you will get a first class compartment, all to yourself."

At this, the woman smiled. "I most certainly hope so."

Betty looked at Ellen, smiled wryly as her younger sister pulled her to her for warmth.

The lorry drove past the station entrance, entered the goods yard, where it stopped. The driver undid the canvas flap, but before he could let down the tailboard, a loud, officious voice called out to him, "What the hell do you think you are doing?"

The driver answered, "They are Jews for deportation, sir, we were told to head for the goods yard and - ."

The first voice cut him off, "I know that, you idiot, they are late and you are supposed to bring them to the train. Go left here, you should see the wagons after about a kilometre."

The driver climbed back into his cab, apologising, "Yes, sir, sorry sir."

The lorry drove on over the rough, uneven goods yard. One of the young men sitting next to Ellen leaned out of the rear. He sat back down saying, "It seems we are not the only ones here."

Ellen peered around the edge, she looked at the scene. Her heart sank as she saw the hundreds of people, gathered by a long line of cattle wagons coupled to a steam engine.

As the lorry drove by, Ellen and the others saw armed soldiers herding men, women, and children up wooden ramps into cattle trucks using their rifles as clubs on the protesting few.

The well-dressed woman pushed her way through to the rear of the truck, looked at the crowds as they drove past, "They must be criminals," While holding onto her hat she peered around the side of the lorry. She turned to the others. "Where's our train, I can't see it?"

The same old man from before, told her, "It's probably been detained, so it looks like we will be joining these, er, criminals as you call them."

The truck came to a halt, shunting them forward for one last time, and a voice rang out, "Out, out you swine, move it, move it."

The tailboard lowered along with a crash. Everyone climbed down, amidst the shouts and curses, onto the wet cobblestones. One of the elderly men slipped, fell to his knees, groaning. An army officer, with the SS insignia on his collar, kicked him in the ribs, causing him to collapse in a heap. He turned to two men. "Pick him up, get in line with the others." The men complied in haste, joining the others as soldiers formed them into rows.

The driver approached the officer and handed him a list, he stood to attention and said, "Thirty-two deportees, sir."

The officer turned to an NCO, "Thirty, two, Sergeant, count them." He looked at the driver, "You can keep an eye on them while he does it."

Ellen helped Betty to climb down, and stumbled as one of the soldiers pushed her, cursing her and her companions, "Get in line, we have to count you." He screamed at the others still inside the truck, "Move it, Jewish scum, get out of the vehicle."

With the counting over, Ellen walked on, supporting Betty, who grimaced with each step. A soldier raised his rifle butt threateningly, Ellen quickened their pace, joining the crowd at the end of a long row of parked lorries.

Ellen looked around at the people milling outside the cattle trucks, all of them frightened and confused as they waited. The children were the most affected by the shouting, and the cries of the injured. Almost every single one of them was crying, and some of them, separated from their parents, called out plaintively, lost amongst the commotion.

Ellen managed to stay with Betty at the rear of the crowd, listening, hoping to pick up some information about their journey.

Several people called out plaintively, "Where are you taking us, what have we done wrong, we are not criminals?"

Most of these questions were answered either with a kick

from a jack-booted foot or a blow from a rifle butt.

The loading continued and the soldiers threw those who fell off the wooden ramp, whether injured or not, inside the next available wagon.

David.

Standing behind Ellen and her sister, quite close to the lorry, young David Stein, 16, and his younger brother looked to their companions, he pointed to a red brick building some way off and said, "I'm going to make a run for it, to that building over there, it's out of the line of sight of most of the guards, but we must go one at a time, once one of us is there, then the next one can follow, and when it's dark we can slip away."

He slipped away from the crowd, hid at the rear of the lorry, then sprinted over to a large rail yard building, over two hundred away, its huge doors closed and padlocked. His brother, Simon, was next, he made it unnoticed, the next one followed, then suddenly, the dozen young men waiting for their turn, lost patience or maybe it was fear that spurned them, as they broke away and ran off after the others.

The noise caused as they ran helter-skelter over the cobbles attracted the attention of one of the children, she said aloud, dancing about, pointing with her outstretched arm, in all innocence before her mother could stop her, "Look Mummy, Mummy, they don't want to come with us, where are they going to? Can we go -."

The driver, leaning against the lorry's radiator, heard the child, he shouldered his rifle and ran round to the rear of his vehicle, and seeing the last of the young men disappearing around the barn, gave the alarm, "Attention, attention, they're running away, over there, by the siding shed," and gave pursuit.

The SS officer in charge of loading blew his whistle several times, alerting all the guards in the compound and screamed at the guards standing by the cattle trucks, "Get after them you fools, follow him."

An NCO called out to his men as he ran with in the same direction, "Don't let them get away, or we'll be facing Ivan, and winter's on its way."

The guards at the main gate, alerted by the commotion, moved towards the railway building.

Ellen watched anxiously as the soldiers chased after the

young men. She saw more soldiers, stationed at the goods yard periphery, closing in on the building where the youths were hiding. She watched as the SS officer in charge ran in the same direction with three more men armed with machine pistols.

David groaned in frustration as he saw the soldiers, "I knew it," he gasped to his brother, "I should have taken you and left the others, I hoped they would stay calm. How wrong I was."

He shook his head as the others gathered around him, looking at him in confusion, in desperation and fear, "Why did you not wait, we could have made it, going one at a time, now we are all in for a beating."

The soldiers arrived, cursing, "Yiddish scum, do you think we have nothing better to do." The young men stood with their backs up against the brick wall of the siding shed, surrounded by two dozen armed and angry soldiers.

The soldiers moved in on them, rifle butts jabbing, bruising flesh; then the boots, studded with metal, heels in ribcages, in groins and when possible in faces, then the rifle butts once more until the youths lay bleeding, bruised on the ground.

The sergeant in charge of the group, called out, "That's

enough boys that should teach these shitty Jews not to run away." Then he said, "Now, on your feet, Jewish scum."

The SS officer from the train came running up, shouted at the sergeant after catching his breath, "What the hell do you think you are doing you imbecile?"

David looked on in dazed surprise; he thought the sergeant was in trouble for hitting them.

The sergeant stood there open-mouthed. "Sir, they were trying to escape."

The SS officer took out his pistol. David thought he was going to shoot one of his own men. The officer said quietly while watching the NCO, "I know that you cretin, you are wasting time, so shoot them."

David looked at the others in fear and back at the sergeant, the NCO's mouth dropped open once more, then he said, "Shoot them, sir?"

The officer shook his head in derision, cocked his pistol, and said, "Yes, like this." He pointed his gun and fired three times, each bullet shattering the skull of one of David's companions. The officer turned to the three SS soldiers, armed with machine pistols, who had accompanied him, "You three, shoot them."

The sergeant and half-a-dozen soldiers from the driving element, consisting of men over forty, moved quickly out of the way, watching dumfounded as the three soldiers fired their weapons without hesitation into the remaining youths, not stopping until the firing pins hit an empty chamber.

David felt nothing except a hard kick in the chest, then darkness.

The officer examined the bodies. He looked down at David who awoke from a fading dream, peered through a red mist at the pistol pointing at his head, then he fell, quickly, gratefully, into a deep black hole.

Ellen heard shouting, then she heard several shots, then the hammering sound of machinegun fire, followed by several more gunshots, then silence. She turned back to the waiting people in disbelief, standing there ashen-faced, then Betty came to her, took her in her arms.

Someone said, "They've shot those poor boys," and one woman fainted, caught in time by her husband.

Then someone else said, "They wouldn't dare."

Above the murmuring and doubtful tones, an old man said, "Well that wasn't chamber music you just heard, that was a couple of Schmeissers, machine pistols." He turned to the group of soldiers, said, "Look, the arseholes are coming back and those boys aren't with them."

The SS officer and his men arrived back, the loading continued, accompanied by shouts and curses, with the guards now keeping a watchful eye on the crowd.

As the last cattle truck filled up, soldiers pulled the gangplank away, slid the door shut and dropped the latch.

Ellen and Betty stood with a shocked crowd of about six dozen others; they looked at each other in fear, their future uncertain after the shootings.

The officer turned to them, shaking his head in disgust. "We're a carriage short; I knew there were too many." He motioned to the armed soldiers behind him with his arms; they quickly formed a semi-circle in front of the crowd, facing inwards. He turned to the sound of motor vehicles, he motioned to his men, "Wait, we have company, let them pass first, we don't need an audience."

Chapter Nine.

Intervention.

Colonel Bernard von Nordhausen leaned forward, peering between the driver and Major Platt. He saw soldiers armed with machine pistols herding a large group of people together, "Another trainload of deportees, the poor devils."

He imagined it had something to do with the recent gunfire they'd heard in the distance as they had set off at the head of the column. Everyone knew of the transportation of Jews to the work camps in Poland. He sat back with a sigh, staring forward, his face wrought with pity, and he thought of Melanie, his wife, back home in Berlin.

He broke off his apathy abruptly as the General nudged him. "What's the matter Bernard?" The general, curious, and noticing his concern, peered around the driver at the cattle wagons, the crowd of people, the soldiers, saying, "What is that ahead?"

Nordhausen told him, "The Jews sir, deportation to work camps in Poland, it seems they have quite a few left over, I believe they are going to shoot them."

The General nodded, "Yes, I have heard of it, something like a hundred to a truck, the poor buggers." He leaned forward, "Driver, pull up at the bend."

Ellen, standing at the edge of the crowd, turned as three Kubelwagens halted on the road near to her.

Behind two dozen half-track army vehicles, a long column of trucks came to a stop. The general stood up, looked at the crowd of frightened people. He said quietly to the SS officer, "What are you doing Lieutenant?"

The SS officer stiffened to attention, raised his arm, called out, "Heil Hitler."

The general ignored him asked once more, "I said what are you doing Lieutenant?"

The SS man stuttered, "We, we, er, are transporting Jews to the labour camps, Herr General."

The general looked at the scene, the packed cattle carriages, "On foot, maybe?"

"The wagons are full, Herr General."

The general pointed to several larger, dilapidated freight wagons standing farther down the line, "Use one of those freight wagons."

The officer shook his head adamantly, "My orders were to fill these cattle trucks with these people and they are now full, Herr General."

The general stepped out of the vehicle with one of his aides, a Major, "We are at war Lieutenant, and my orders to you are, put these Jews aboard that freight car, now."

The lieutenant said, "But...!" and he stopped as the general's aide whipped out his pistol, pointed it at him.

The general said, "Refusing to obey a direct order will result in your immediate execution, Jews or no Jews."

The lieutenant turned, screamed at his men, "You lot, go and bring that freight wagon here at the double and couple it up."

A dozen soldiers ran off towards the freight car. After a few minutes it joined the long line of cattle trucks; in the meantime, a small group of officers from the other open-topped vehicles had joined the general.

The general asked him, "What is your name Lieutenant?"

"Rotz, Herr General."

Someone in the group of soldiers sniggered, the general said, while hiding a smile, "I heard shooting earlier on, Rotz, what was that about?" He glanced briefly at the siding shed.

Rotz swallowed dryly, "Some of them tried to escape, Herr General, they offered resistance."

"Were they armed?"

Rotz shook his head quickly, "No sir, but they refused to return to the train and the trains must run on time, I had no choice."

Nordhausen approached, he whispered at length to the General. The general raised his eyebrows and spoke to Rotz in Russian, "The Fuhrer will be proud to hear that, a dedicated warrior, not afraid to carry out his duty."

Rotz straightened up stiffly, answered in perfect Russian, "Thank you, Herr General."

The general turned to Nordhausen, spoke with him quietly at length; he in turn, smiling, turned to another officer who had joined him from the second vehicle.

After speaking with him, he watched as the man marched off briskly to one of the larger transport vehicles, then Nordhausen and the general watched as soldiers set a gangplank in place. He looked upon the small crowd of people carrying their hand luggage, men, women and children, the yellow Star of David vividly displayed on the back and front of their clothing.

He heard a baby cry and then saw a middle-aged woman helping another, older woman, climb the ramp. She turned and looked at him and smiled her thanks, and then she followed the others up into the wagon. As she stepped inside, the soldiers made to remove the ramp, she turned around as Nordhausen shouted aloud, "Don't forget about sanitation, Lieutenant Rotz, and water, or do you want them to die of thirst. Germany needs these people, these labourers, for the glory of the Third Reich, is that not so?"

The SS officer said, "These people don't know the meaning of sanitation, they-." He faltered as the Major undid his holster flap and rested his hand on the pistol butt while observing him intently. Rotz nodded, "Yes, Herr Colonel, of course."

He turned to a sergeant. "You heard the order, bring water, and bring those, er, empty drums too." He indicated two medium-sized oil drums cleanly sawn in half, used for drainage purposes. The sergeant ran off shouting orders, he returned with his men, the two rusty drums, and half a dozen buckets of water, taken gratefully by the occupants.

The soldiers strained with the sliding door, the wheels screeching in annoyance as they closed the heavy wooding frame. Eventually the truck door closed.

General climbed back into his vehicle with the others.

The SS officer waved his hand and with the couplings clanking, the train pulled slowly away.

On Rotz's orders, the drivers and soldiers climbed into the trucks.

The General called out to Rotz before he could make his departure and said, "Lieutenant Rotz, we leave for the Russian front tomorrow, Colonel von Nordhausen has informed me of your previous occupation, an interpreter. You speak Russian, French, and English and I am in desperate need of a translator of your high calibre, and especially someone with your tenacity. Give your particulars to my adjutant, then go with him and collect your things."

Rotz stood there, uncertain. The general smiled along with the colonel and said, "Don't worry, my little 'Sonder Staffel' hero, your commanding officer is a very good friend of mine. I'll have your transfer arranged to the SS detachment under my command in no time; this could of course mean promotion." He added. "You will like Russia, lots of snow and lots of Russians. Now move it."

Chapter Ten.

The Journey.

Ellen peered around her, after a while her eyes became accustomed to the gloom. The carriage, old well-used, rocked from side to side. There was enough room for half the occupants to sit down on the rough wooden floor. Most of these were women and elderly men.

Ellen guided Betty to a small upturned box, eased her down. She said, "Can you smell that, what is it?"

Betty said, "Cow dung, they must have used this to transport cattle, look, there, improvised ventilation." She pointed upwards to several small holes high up near the ceiling at the front and back.

Ellen looked at the rough wooden floor after her shoe caught on a splinter. A young girl standing next to her wheezed heavily, gasping for breath. Ellen asked her, "Are you alright?"

The girl, around sixteen, nodded, managed to say, "Asthma."

"Are you alone here?"

The girl nodded.

"Where are your parents?"

She answered with a movement of her head towards the front end of the truck.

"Here?"

She shook her head.

Ellen pulled her to her. "They are in another truck I take it?"

The girl nodded once more.

A young man, steadying his wife as she held their baby, called out, "Where they are taking us."

Someone muttered, "Does it matter."

An old Rabbi said, "Well wherever it is, it is certainly not the promised land."

A voice called out, "What, no milk and honey, looks like I will have to go on a diet."

Ellen thought of the young men who had ran off, and she tried to understand why they had died.

After two hours travel, the train slowed abruptly. The truck lurched, crashing against the buffers of the truck in front, jolting as the other shunted it back, shuttling the occupants back and forth, causing several elderly people to fall.

As the train slowed gradually down to a stop, the occupants murmured quietly, someone, a man, asked in his misery, "Are we there already?"

Another man said bitterly, "You ask if we are there, why do you ask, do you know where we are heading?"

The somewhat subdued answer came back, "No, I don't."

The other replied, "Then don't ask."

A woman, cried out, "They are going to shoot us," started wailing.

In the total blackness, the children, some of them held clear of the cold wooden floor by their parents or some kind stranger, on hearing the woman's cries, whimpered in fear.

There was relief all round as a man near the doorway, his ear to the wall said, "No. They are changing the guards, nothing more."

The truck lurched, forwards, then back again. People staggered and fell to the floor, cursing loudly. After one heavy shuddering movement forward, the train continued on its journey, everyone sighed with relief as it kept on going, slowly picking up speed, on their way once more.

As the dilapidated truck rattled over the rails, and the hours went by, the smell of machine oil and cow dung, from the earlier contents of the freight wagon, dissipated, replaced by the smell of human urine. An old woman lying with her back against the wall called out to Ellen as she passed on her way from the 'toilet', "My husband, he will not wake up."

Ellen edged closer, the woman held a frail old man to her. Ellen looked at his still form, called for her sister, "Betty, this man, I think he is ill."

Betty joined her, stopped and placed her fingers on the man's neck. She checked his breathing. She squeezed his ear hard, but the old man stayed still. She rose up looked at Ellen, sighed and whispered, "His pulse is there and he is breathing. I think he has suffered a stroke. There is nothing we can do." She turned to the old woman and said quietly, "He is sleeping, he is suffering from exhaustion." The old woman, satisfied, pulled the pitiful bundle closer to her.

Ellen looked down at them. "This shouldn't be happening; there is something horribly wrong here."

During the daylong journey and into the night, almost everybody emptied their bladder in the containers provided.

As the black night continued, the odorous smell of human faeces permeated throughout the truck as several of the occupants defecated in the containers, while the others held on.

Ellen looked at her sister and moved closer to her, "What about the people in the other trucks, do you think they have toilets?"

Betty shook her head and whispered, "You are so naïve Ellen, tell me, what do you think?"

"They gave us buckets to use; I imagine the other people will have the same or perhaps something bigger."

"Yes, Ellen, they probably have," she said

The train moved on relentlessly through the night, in the eerie darkness the bodies swayed like human waves with the movement of the train, and children slept either in their parent's or in other arms.

Ellen, holding on to her sister, fought to stay awake with her. The cold penetrated her overcoat, she stood up, pulling Betty up with her. "We must keep moving, our circulation, we must stay warm. Come now, do as I do."

In the cramped space, they stamped their feet to increase their circulation, and joining hands pushed and pulled gently, while several others copied them. They continued until they were out of breath, then Ellen looked at Betty. "How do you feel now?"

Betty nodded, "Better, warmer, but thirsty."

Ellen said, "Come with me then."

They searched around the wagon, pushing through the tightly packed bodies; they found the water buckets eventually; all six were empty.

The train stopped once, to take on water and fuel for the engine, after which it lurched onwards at high speed, as if wanting to bring to an end this journey of death.

The hours dragged by through the long cold day and the following night.

Ellen, half dozing, while propped up against the wall with Betty, woke as someone screamed. Betty, asked her groggily, "What is-, I heard someone at the door, shall-?"

A loud wailing interrupted her, and a woman called out above the noise; "Her baby is dead, the poor thing."

A baby lay dead in its mother's arms. It was a young woman, sobbing, with no husband to care for her. An elderly woman went to her, spoke words of comfort while embracing her and the baby.

Ellen edged over to the old woman, still crouched down, clinging to her husband's inert body. Ellen checked his pulse, the skin ice cold to the touch, and found none. The old man who had suffered a seizure earlier had now passed on peacefully in his wife's arms.

Ellen and Betty cried along with the others as the Rabbi called out the prayers for the dead.

Gradually, the stench of human faeces and urine increased, making the air inside the truck almost un-breathable.

The old woman passed away unnoticed, still holding onto her husband's lifeless body.

That same night, Ellen comforted the asthmatic sixteen-year-old girl, whose name was Rachel, she guided her to the upturned toolbox and sat her down, she crouched down next to her and pulled her to her, listening to her soft wheezing as the girl gradually succumbed to sleep.

Some hours later, Betty woke Ellen; she had fallen asleep while still holding Rachel. She looked at the girl sleeping peacefully, then she noticed the still body, the absence of that gentle wheeze. Ellen wept as more prayers followed.

With her eyes swollen from countless tears, Ellen, squashed up in a corner, leaned once more against her sister, for shared warmth, her eyes gradually became heavy in spite of the cold flooring, but thanks to the vibrations and the loud, continuous noise of the metal wheels, clack-clack, clack-clack -- clack-clack, clack-clack, she eventually drifted off to sleep.

A pencil thin shaft of sunlight shone through one of the small holes in the roof, played on Ellen's left eyelid, waking her. She stretched painfully, peered through the gloom. To her it seemed they had been travelling for an age, and she was thirsty, just like the other passengers.

As she took a deep breath, she gagged, her breath caught. She peered at the toilet drums nearby, and saw one of them lying on its side. The liquid contents had seeped through the floorboards leaving the faeces exposed to the air.

Rising stiffly to her feet, she shook Betty roughly awake while breathing through her handkerchief, trying to ignore the stench, picking up their tiny suitcases.

As Betty rose up someone took their places on the box. Ellen made her way with her through the swaying mass towards the doorway as more sunlight strayed through the tiny gaps there.

Ellen stumbled and fell as she tripped over several inert bodies, as she reached out to save herself, her hand accidentally touched a face, thinking its owner was asleep, she whispered "sorry," then recoiled as she recognised the feel of death.

She rose up with Betty's help stepped over other men or women lying there asleep, dead, or maybe dying. She embraced her sister, who was looking at her in despair, "Don't give in now, Betty, it will soon be over." She hugged her to her fiercely. *'Oh dear God, why is this happening to us?'*

They made it across the crowded carriage, saw an elderly man sucking in air through a small opening in the rotted wood.

He looked round at her as she inched her way to him dragging an unwilling Betty with her. He moved to one side, allowing them to crouch by the hole. She closed her lips around it and the thoughts flooded her mind as she breathed in. Oh, how sweet it tastes, like honey, like fresh cool water on a hot day.

After giving Betty her turn she peered through the opening. She could see the steam engine as it approached the outskirts of a large city on a long curve.

The man asked as the truck clattered over points, their speed reducing, "Are we there yet, do you know where we're going?" He sounded tired, gasping as he breathed.

Ellen peered at the landscape through the small hole, looking for something recognisable; all she could see were fields, the occasional tree, farm buildings. She felt lost, insecure, but still hoped for the best. She said to the man, "I have no idea, how far have we travelled, what have you seen?"

His face was pale, dark around the eyes, he answered weakly, "We've passed through Berlin, that's about two hundred kilometres. We should have covered another two hundred in the night, this train has been really moving along between stops," he stopped for breath then said, "We even moved in daylight like we are doing now, so we must be out of Germany, safe from enemy aircraft."

She peered through the crack saw a sign. She said aloud, "We are now passing through...Posen, wherever that may be."

The old man looked around him, excited, "We are in Poland. We might be stopping here for food and water."

A weakened voice not far behind them said, "Oh that's good, I am feeling rather peckish after missing breakfast, lunch, dinner, and supper for the last two, or was it three or maybe four, or even five days."

The old man laughed, coughed, then he winced, his face screwed up in pain. As the train picked up speed he leaned against the side of the truck sighed softly and closed his eyes.

Ellen smiled and turned away from the hole, allowing her sister to take her place once more and she hoped the treatment meted out so far was not an indication of their future.

The train slowed after a good hour's ride, the occupants called out in relief as the locomotive's whistle blew. Their truck crashed against buffers of the one in front, shunting it several times in quick succession as it bounced back and forth causing spillage from the other oil drum. The truck rolled on swaying from side to side, the wooden walls creaking, groaning as the train passed over a number of points, with the undercarriage rattling alarmingly.

Although one or two people complained, the rest kept quiet, as most of them were too tired to utter even a whimper.

The train slowed some more, its brakes squealing, as if protesting against its destination. With a final bone-shaking crash, the train halted. One of the water buckets used as a toilet, tipped over, the contents, mostly urine, spread over the floor, leaked away through the cracks in the wood - but nobody cared.

More shouts, more banging on the sides of the truck, more screams, children crying, soldiers swearing, and dogs barking, then the door opened with a crash, followed by shouts of, "Out, out you pigs, move yourselves," and blinded by the light the occupants clambered, jumped, or half-fell out the truck, hungry, thirsty; above all, afraid.

Ellen looked down at the old man they had found by the hole, took his arm as he stared past her vacantly. Betty nudged her, removed her hand gently, saying, "Leave him be, he has passed on, poor fellow, like the others."

Ellen turned and looked numbly at the truck floor in the light from the doorway, she gasped at the sight. She counted more bodies lying amongst the human waste products. The woman whose baby had died sat in the corner with slashed wrists, the blood on her skin, dried black, while her baby lay with its tiny arms outstretched on her lap. Rachel sat curled up in the corner with her body resting against the toolbox where they had left her.

Ellen and Betty climbed down onto the platform where they gathered in a huddle, the smell of urine and human faeces filled the air; the looks on the soldier's faces was enough indication of their condition, as they stepped back well away from them.

Over a dozen soldiers held German shepherd guard dogs barking furiously, on long leashes, their handlers enjoying the looks of terror, the frightened cries of the women and children.

They shouted in feigned anger, "Move on you pigs," allowing the dogs to close in on the unfortunates before pulling them back.

Someone sniggered and said. "Look at the state of em'; they've been wallowin' in their own shit as usual."

"What a stink."

"Situation normal."

"Who's goin' to have to clean the truck out, then?"

Answered by another snigger. "The Poles, who else."

A voice called out, this time from the cattle wagon's doorway, "We've got ten dead here, eleven, counting a baby."

Another soldier, a corporal, approached as the other spoke, told him irritably, "Eleven, is that all, there's at least two dozen dead in each of the others, which means burial detail again, damn Jews."

A sergeant approached, bellowed at them, "Stop moaning and go and get those bloody Polish shirkers, these trains have to run on time, no daylight runs in the Fatherland anymore, thanks to the RAF and Goering, the stupid twat."

The corporal rushed off, the others herded Ellen's group along the platform.

Ellen, her joints stiff and while supporting Betty, staggered on with the others as they made their way towards a line of waiting trucks. One young woman, weeping, asked aloud, "Where is my husband, where are we, where are you taking us?"

An SS officer, although standing upwind, a handkerchief held delicately over his mouth, said irritably, "To the employment centre at Litzmannstadt in Poland, your place of work, now move it, into the lorries you filthy, stinking pigs."

Ellen and Betty with the help of the younger men climbed in and sat down on the floor of one of the trucks.

Betty stared at Ellen, her face blank and said quietly. "Hurrah, work at last."

Chapter Eleven.

Litzmannstadt/Lotzd.

They stood there, packed together, tired and weary, half-frozen, swaying in unison, their movements determined by the vehicle's progress.

The wind blew through the gaps in the canvas covering. The old people groaned, children called out, while the others suffered in silence.

Ellen held onto one of the vehicles stays with one hand and Betty with the other. A young woman clung to them both, sobbing, calling out to her husband or brother, "Joachim, Joachim, where are you?"

Forced to endure the journey over pot-holed roads, heavy jolts brought the old and infirm to their knees, some climbed to their feet, while others stayed where they lay too tired to care.

After two hours of torture, the vehicle braked heavily, shuddering to a stop, greeted by shouts of, "Wake up you lazy bastards, out, out." The rear flap drew back, the tailgate crashed down, "Out you idle scum, out, out you Yiddish filth."

Some of them fell from the vehicle, or fell as they hit the uneven ground.

Ellen half-climbed down and held out her arms for Betty, but someone inside the lorry shoved her and Ellen caught her as she fell, and unable to hold her they both hit the ground together.

With her head spinning, Ellen rose ungainly to her feet and helped Betty, who groaned aloud, to a sitting position, then helped her stand up.

The soldiers, members of the SS, screamed at them continually, pushing them with their rifle butts.

"Baba, Baba!"

A young girl of around twelve left the crowd, her arms outstretched, walking slowly over the rough ground. She passed a group of soldiers; one of them waved his hand in front of her face to no effect.

"She's blind." One of them exclaimed.

Another one laughed, "A blind Jew!"

"Worthless!" said another.

A soldier neared her and shouted, "Boo!" in her ear.

The child faltered momentarily, and then stumbled on, "Baba, Baba!"

"She's deaf too" he said.

"Deaf, dumb and blind, she's more than worthless."

One of the soldiers stuck his foot out, tripping the girl, who fell to the ground, "Oops," he called out grinning, while his comrades laughed.

The girl, on her hands and knees called out even louder, "Baba, Baba, Babaaa."

An officer approached the group, tall and gaunt in appearance, with a swarthy complexion, "Have you lot nothing better to do?" He looked at the girl, "What's the matter with her?"

"She's blind, sir," said one soldier

"And deaf," quipped another.

The officer took out his pistol, loaded it and shot the girl in the face as she rose. A cloud of blood erupted from the back of her head as it jerked back, knocking her to the ground

A woman rushed out of the crowd, screaming, "My baby, you've shot my baby," and fell to her knees, crushing the girl's body to her.

The officer raised his pistol and fired once more.

Ellen and the rest of the throng stood in shocked silence, staring at the man and the two lifeless forms.

He raised his pistol, "Are there any more misfits amongst you?"

The crowd of people averted their eyes, turned away in numbed silence.

A soldier screamed, "Move out, you lot, over the road with you."

From where they stood amongst the crowd, Ellen and Betty saw a huge compound, containing four-to-five storey accommodation blocks, factory buildings, bordered as far as the eye could see in both directions by wooden fencing, covered thickly with coiled barbed wire.

This was Ghetto Lodz, the part of a city renamed Litzmannstadt in honour of a WWI General.

The entrance to this place was over a roughly constructed wooden bridge. The crowd moved quickly, urged on by angry and impatient soldiers. As they entered the compound a scene of horror greeted them. Men, women, and children, dirty and emaciated, most of them dressed in rags, stared at the newcomers. A number of children trudged towards them with outstretched hands.

A woman called out in horror, recoiling as one child, its skin stretched over its face, eyes surrounded by dark patches, sunk inside its skull, touched her clothing, "Oh, dear God preserve us."

Ellen said, "Oh my God, look at them, what do they want?"

Betty said aloud, "Food, what else?"

A woman close behind them said, "Food, who can think of food at a time like this, give me water, just water, I've been drinking my husband's urine for the past two days."

The children pestered them silently, then several men came forward, the clothes they wore were clean, they appeared well-fed. They pushed the children roughly to one side; one of the unfortunates stumbled, fell, then lay still and the man who had caused the child to fall, hooked his foot under the frail carcass, heaved it unceremoniously to one side, leaving it where it lay in the gutter staring dark-eyed to the heavens.

Ellen called out, "Why did-."

The man turned on her, eyes hard, "Shut it, and keep moving."

They followed the long line of people, the men, women, and children from the train, towards a doorway; watched over by two dozen more men wearing black armbands carrying the inscription KAPO (camp police) on them in white block lettering.

They came to an official-looking building. At the doorway, a kapo instructed them to remove any items of soiled clothing, leave them outside and have their passes ready.

They filed inside with the others, approached a table where two civilians sat. Ellen holding Betty upright with the help of one of the younger men.

As their turn came, Betty, standing in front her with her eyes screwed shut, failed to move. Ellen urged her forward. Betty had her pass ready, handed it over. One of the men took it, read aloud to his colleague who sat with his pen in his hand as he hunched over a ledger, writing down the spoken details.

"Holstein, Betty, single, aged 57. - Next." He threw her pass into a wooden crate, already half-full.

Ellen moved forward promptly, handed over her pass. Without looking at her face, the man snatched it, said, "Kaempfer nee Holstein, Ellen, married, 47." The man looked up at her, then at the women behind her. He frowned. "You are married to a German citizen, where is he?"

Ellen looked at the pimple-faced man. "I'm divorced; it says so in my pass."

He looked once more at the pass in his hand. He reddened slightly, threw it into the crate with the others, then he saw the gold wedding ring on her right hand. "Well, you won't need that then."

He leaned forward quickly, grabbed her right hand, pulled her forward. He seized her ring finger, she winced as he removed it, dropped it into his side pocket, she heard it jingle as it joined others. He looked up at her, said, "Move on then. Next!"

They joined a queue to the next table, at which two more civilians sat. One of them asked her, "Have you ever used a sewing machine?"

Ellen nodded, "Yes, I make my own dresses."

He looked at Betty, "What about you?"

"I have on occasion used one."

He looked to the kapo standing near to them, "Put them with the others." He looked at Ellen. "This is a camp policeman, do what he tells you."

Ellen asked, "May we have something to drink please, we have had nothing for days."

The man at the table stared at her blankly, the kapo pushed them away then led them to a group of women like themselves, standing behind a table. He growled as Ellen turned to him, "You will keep your mouth shut. Now, open your cases."

They laid their cases on the table and opened them.

They both watched helplessly as half a dozen men searched through their things. They took their perfume, talcum powder, tooth powder, most of their toilet soap and a bottle of disinfectant Betty had brought with her.

Ellen thought of the package she gave to Elfriede.

They closed their cases, received ration cards for food, informed they could keep the rest of their toiletries, then they were moved away from the table to wait with the others.

After this illegal confiscation, the registration by the two civilians, Jews like herself; Ellen and her sister watched as the other people were sorted out, young, old, single males, single females and families.

Ellen noticed to her relief the absence of German soldiers, everywhere.

The man with the black and white armband came to them, "Over there," he said. He ushered her, Betty, and a bunch of other women to another room containing a large stone sink.

Betty said quietly, "Water, thank God."

Ellen and her sister waited their turn at the water taps, where they gratefully drank until they thought their stomachs would burst. They washed themselves as best they could in the crowded room, drying their hands and faces on the towels taken from their luggage.

They settled down on the bare floor with the others. As Ellen looked around her she became aware of the fact that she was one of the eldest of the thirty or so females packed in there, then she lay back and fell asleep.

***

"Get up, on your feet, wake up, stand up, and get your things. You have to move out of here."

Ellen felt somebody shaking her; she rose from the fog and saw Betty tugging at her coat. "Come dear, we have to go." She stood up with the rest of the women, picked up her small suitcase and looked around the room.

A bunch of kapo's pulled the other women to their feet, pushed them towards the door. She went with them holding Betty steady as she stumbled.

They left the building, joined the others, all of them now in their groups, single men in one, single women in another, with a third group consisting of men, women, and children. Someone called out, pointing down the roadway, "Move on, stay in line and no talking." The crowd moved off slowly, traipsing along the road.

As they reached a junction, Ellen's group turned right as instructed, leaving the other groups as they carried on.

They continued along the dusty thoroughfare, stopped outside a huge apartment block. A ghetto police officer, holding a clipboard, called out to them as he stood on the pavement, while indicating the building behind him, "Here is your new accommodation; cooking and bathing facilities are in the basement. Now remember this address. This is number two, Richterstrasse. Come forward when I call your name. You will be given an apartment number. You will enter this building and go to this apartment. There you will leave your belongings, and then return to the street. Then you will wait until you are collected and brought to your place of work."

Ellen looked at Betty. "At last, our new home and a place to work."

Betty looked at her, but said nothing and they listened to the man with the others as he called out names and apartment numbers, then the group moved on to the next doorway.

As they arrived at number nine, they heard their names called, and the apartment, number eleven.

They left the small group of women and walked through the opening, Ellen could not help noticing the absence of a door.

Inside, standing by the main staircase, another kapo said, "Apartment number?"

Ellen told him, "Number eleven."

"Up the stairs, first floor, turn right, it's the last door but one on your left."

Jostled by the crowd behind them, Betty stumbled, Ellen lifted her arm onto her shoulder, and they made their way up the well-worn wooden stairway.

On reaching the top, they followed the kapo's directions, arrived at a doorway, with the number eleven scratched in the plaster next to it. They looked around them as they entered. There were no windows in the cold and damp room, just two double-tiered bunk beds with straw mattresses, no sanitation except for an old enamel bucket, no water.

Betty, leaning for support against one of the bunks said sardonically, "Oh, how wonderful, just what I needed for my arthritis." She turned to Ellen, "Where do you think the toilet and the bathroom is?"

"The man said it was in the basement."

Two young women entered behind them, one said, "Hello, my name is Sarah and this is Ruth."

Ruth said as she saw the beds, "It looks like we are sharing."

Ellen searched in the dimness with her hands above her head; then she found a light switch on the wall, tried it without success. "It appears we have no lighting."

Betty's voice rang out, "Well that's something less to pay for."

They left their luggage in one corner, walked back to the stairway along with their roommates, descended the stairs onto the street.

Outside, they joined the main group once more; saw a man dressed in expensive clothes standing next to a civilian automobile. The kapos' moved them off along the road, with the man following in his Mercedes.

The journey, on foot, took them the best part of half an hour and on the way there, to their horror, they saw frequently, gangs of emaciated children roaming the street, running off as soon as they spotted them.

Ellen looked on in repulsion as three other children, dressed in tattered rags, their gender unknown because of their shaven heads, stumbled after a sewer rat. Their skinny legs, unfortunately, were no match for the rodent, they had not the strength to move their frail bodies any faster than a meagre trot, and the fortunate creature disappeared down a nearby drain.

One woman said to another, "My god, did you see that, those kids were chasing a rat, I do believe they were going to eat it if they caught it, did you see how thin they were?"

One of the kapos' called out, "Don't be so choosy, there's a lot of meat on one of those things, the little buggers do rather well from the cemetery." After which there followed anxious murmurs and whispers from the group as they trudged on.

Betty was tiring as Ellen's group turned a corner and came upon two men, less than fifty metres farther on, kicking another man as he lay on the ground. He was holding to a small object clutched tightly to his chest. A woman in the crowd called out, "Somebody do something. They are hurting him."

One of the kapos' shouted at the men as they stamped on the other's head. One of the assailants relieved their victim of the object, a loaf of bread, laughing as they ran off with it.

Two of the kapos' approached the fallen man, one of them examined him, rose up shaking his head, "He's had it, he's dead."

The Factory.

After a while, with the scenes from her journey still vivid in her mind, Ellen, holding Betty to her, looked ahead at a dark red-brick building hoping this was their destination. The kapo, half-turned his head, saying aloud, "There it is, your place of work."

They stopped at an open doorway; noise came from the stairway inside. They filed in after one of their escorts, climbing the stairs in pairs.

After walking down a long, dimly lit corridor, they entered a huge room. There stood row upon row of industrial sewing machines, half of them in use.

As soon as they entered, the machine noise stopped, the kapos' distributed them, one to a machine. With everyone at their place, the well-dressed civilian climbed up onto a chair and spoke to them.

His voice carried along the length of the room, "This is my factory, you are my workers, I have a monthly quota to fill, which means you have a daily quota to fill and you will see to it that this quota is filled. The machines are easy to use, so learn quickly. You will be sewing blankets, uniforms and other necessary paraphernalia for our brave soldiers. The quality of your work will be strictly, I repeat, strictly controlled, so do not make mistakes, mistakes cost time and money. If you do make a mistake, do not try to hide it or every single one of you will be penalised with loss of pay for that day, money that you will need to buy food."

With his elucidating speech at an end, he motioned to one of the kapos' and said aloud, "It is your and your associates task to see that this lot do their work properly, you know of the consequences don't you?"

The kapo nodded, "Yes, sir."

The well-dressed man stepped down off the chair, and left the room.

In the following hours, after ready-cut material arrived from the cutting room, situated upstairs, the kapo supervisors in the factory showed the uninitiated, how the machines functioned, some learned fast, others, unused to physical labour found it difficult. Betty had trouble with her posture, "If I stay bent over this machine for much longer I'll turn into a bloody hunchback."

Nevertheless, she persevered, learned quickly, whereas Ellen, a hobby dressmaker, had no trouble, she was entrusted with sewing uniform sleeves.

The hours passed slowly at first with no breaks in between.

Darkness came, the work continued until one of the kapos' called a halt. "Finish what you are doing, then tidy up. Then go down stairs, you'll find food there."

As they emerged onto the street, they received a hunk of dried bread, a piece of raw turnip, they took the items wordlessly. The kapo's brought them back to their rooms where they ate and slept.

They wakened the next day; found somebody had stolen their spare underclothing. When they reported the theft the kapo in charge said, "Tough luck, buy new ones in your midday break."

Having no other choice, they bought clothing on the black market as soon as they received their wages, known as ghetto money.

They toiled over noisy machines in a freezing cold building for hours on end. The hours eventually turned into days, with each day starting at six in the morning until eight in the evening. They shopped for food in the ghetto shops after they finished work each night. After eating their frugal meal, they retired gratefully to their beds where they slept an uneasy sleep.

The days stretched into weeks, the weeks into months; each

week new workers came to fill the places left vacant by the poor souls who failed to wake, having died in their sleep or out on the street on their way to or from work.

In their block, the municipal shower, located in the basement, was one overhead faucet providing a pathetic stream of ice-cold water, it was in the same room as one toilet bowl, which flushed weakly, therefore blocked up constantly. The only other supply of water was from a tap in the same room. Then December arrived, bringing with it the frost and snow.

The first morning it snowed heavily they were given shovels, told they must dig their way to the factory through the one and a half meter high snowfall that had drifted, due to high winds, to three meters in height in places.

Ellen and Betty's group, made up mainly of women, were not spared. They toiled over three hours before arriving at their destination. During the day it snowed heavily once again. Work was cut short, everyone left at 4 pm, the snow still falling as they cleared the path once again. Several women fell, exhausted. The kapo's hauled them to their feet, gave them a few minutes rest, then ordered them back to work.

Some didn't make it back four hours later, as those who repeatedly fell were left where they lay.

After a meagre supper of cabbage soup, stale black bread, they undressed for bed, totally exhausted. In the sub-zero room temperature they quickly removed their socks, their outer clothing, taking them with them, sleeping in the same bed, finding it warmer than sleeping alone. It also meant they had double blankets.

Chapter twelve.

December 7th 1941

Hans burst into the apartment room, excited, but unsmiling. The look on his face told Elfriede something was wrong. "The Japanese have bombed Pearl Harbour," he said.

She looked at him, wide-eyed. He added, "It's a large American naval base in the pacific, near to Hawaii. They have caused severe damage to the fleet and I imagine there were many casualties."

She shook her head. "Japan! How could they, what a cowardly thing to do."

"We were just as surprised, but I think the Japs have bitten off more than they can chew, America has a vast fighting machine, their navy, their army and its air force. Not only that, they have the workforce and the experience to use their factories to build more military machines."

She took hold of him as he came to her. "What is going to happen next?"

"I believe this is the start of another world war. The British, who are fighting the japs, have found a much needed ally, an ally filled with much anger and vengeance, at such treachery and we will soon face defeat."

"Defeat, you mean an end to this tyranny," she said.

"Yes, but this mad dog, Hitler, thinks his army is invincible; he thought the same about the Luftwaffe but the Royal Air Force proved him wrong, not only that, things are not going well for us in Russia."

Berlin 1942.

Elfriede watched as he crossed the street, she waited for his footsteps in the hallway. As soon as he entered the room she ran into his arms saying, "I'm pregnant!" His mouth opened slowly, she nodded slowly, said, "Papa."

Lost for words, all he could do was hug her, kiss her. After which he said, "What will be, will be."

She kissed him gently, saying, "If it's a boy I would like to name him after Peter."

"Yes, Peter, our best man, I wonder how he is?"

She rested her head on his shoulder. "His mother wrote to me some time ago, she told me he was serving in Russia. I fear for him, and Robert and young Hans." She looked up at him, "Tell me, where is all this leading too, will our lives ever be the same again?"

He pulled her to him, said quietly, "No, I'm afraid not." He kissed her on the lips. "But I believe things will be better after the war is over, but that will take some time."

Berlin. 1943.

One evening, after their meal, Hans and Elfriede discussed their future, sitting together on the sofa in their well-furnished apartment. He said, "It will be over soon, just you see. It is obvious the Americans and the allies are preparing for an invasion, our positions on the French cast have taken a pasting from the RAF, and their aim has improved tremendously. When the allies land they will be successful and then we will be at peace within a year."

She said, "I wish I had your confidence."

He smiled wryly. "You would have if you were in my shoes, don't forget where I work."

"And how is your work?"

He smiled, "Top secret, I mustn't tell you about the messages the BBC send to the French underground."

She laughed, said, "What messages, secret ones?"

"No, just messages, for example: 'The dog has two tails, but he wags only one of them', or 'My Aunt wears a broad, black hat'."

She laughed. "What do they mean?"

"Nothing to us, but I believe they are camouflage for the real messages."

He added, "The Russians are putting up a fierce resistance, they are pushing towards Poland, and I hope I will be moved out of this city, if I am, you will be coming with me."

She ran her hand slowly over the sofa's leather surface, wriggled her toes in the carpet's thick pile. "I wonder who this apartment belonged to."

"Who do you think?"

She gasped softly, looked at him. "You mean the deportees don't you? Will they get their property back when they return?" She saw the sadness in his eyes. He looked away. She added in the silence, "Did you find out anything about the deportees from Germany, from Hamburg, the ones sent to Poland?"

He looked around the room, his eyes glistening, he spoke, his voice almost a whisper, "I had a word with a new civilian cipher clerk, she'd been working in Frankfurt-am-Maine, when I asked her where she worked he told me 'Lindenstrasse 27'."

Her brow tensed a little, she feared to ask. "What is that," she said.

"Frankfurt Gestapo, headquarters."

"What did she tell you," she said, her fear growing.

He placed an arm around her shoulder. "When I asked her what was to happen to the German Jews deported from Germany, she-." He paused, coughed, cleared his throat, "She broke down, and cried bitterly. She didn't say a word, in fact, she didn't have to. I am afraid your friends may be lost. There is only a slight chance that they will make it."

Her eyes filled with tears as she thought of the package, what it meant to Ellen and herself. "Ellen and Betty, what do you think will happen to them?"

"You mustn't give up hope, they may survive all this," he said and pulled her to him.

Her eyelids fluttered, tears ran. She raised her hands, smeared them across her cheeks. "I read somewhere that hope brings salvation ... hope is all I have now."

They both scrambled to their feet as the sirens sounded, Hans grabbing their overcoats lying ready on the sofa beside him. On their way out, Elfriede picked up Ellen's package from the dresser, hurried with Hans towards the apartment door.

Relocation.

Not only in Berlin, but in other cities as well, the British bombers came at night, the Americans during the day, wreaking devastation, death, injury, bombing the factories, the railway yards, the docks, the housing complexes.

After every all-clear signal, the people of Berlin would emerge from the emergency shelters, gaze in shock at the desolation around them, temporarily lost, some returning to rubble, where once their homes had stood.

With the skies empty of friendly aircraft, the only visible signs of defence against this regular onslaught were the searchlights, the anti-aircraft guns, operated by boys and old men. It was during this terrible period; in 1943, that Peter Thunsdorff saw the light of day.

After a period of devastating attacks, Hans came home at midday, saying, "We are leaving; I have applied for accommodation outside the city." He looked at her, smiling, "You finish feeding Peter, I will start packing, I have transport, we leave immediately."

Elfriede, breast-feeding the baby sighed. "Thank God, I don't think we could survive another night like the last one."

That same afternoon, they left the city centre, moved to Michendorf on the outskirts of Berlin. Elfriede, as usual, carried

Ellen's parcel along with baby Peter, the hope for her friend's safe return still strong in her.

She prayed they would meet once more after all this was over, but as the time dragged by, she began to feel uneasy.

Michendorf

In the following weeks, while sitting in the shelters with Peter, with Ellen's package by her side, Elfriede overheard an old woman talking in subdued tones, *'My boy came home on sick leave yesterday, the stories he told me. They have the Jews penned up in concentration camps; he said he saw lots of dead ones.'*

She heard stories of gibbets and shootings, one old man had winked at her and said, *'Himmler says he has the final solution, you know what that means don't you for the Yids?'* he then drew his finger across his throat and grinned.

She heard a couple discussing the work camps, the deportees, forced to work long hours, with little food. They said the news came from wounded soldiers returning from the front, they'd picked up these stories on their train journey home.

As time went by, she was horrified to hear names of places

where the Nazis exterminated Jews in their thousands, Buchenwald, Bergen Belsen, Auschwitz were names she heard often; she hoped Ellen was far, far away from these places.

Berlin. 1944

On Tuesday evening, the 6th of June, just before midnight, Hans came home late from work, highly excited as he said, "The allies have landed in Normandy; they have broken through the defences and are consolidating. Reports say there are hundreds of thousands of American, British, French, and Canadian troops involved, parachutists and gliders have landed behind the lines and there is confusion everywhere; it seems the Wermacht has been caught with its pants down."

As he held her to him she said, "It was as you said it would be. I wonder how it went for those young men, fighting for freedom, and the others, defending their homeland."

"I don't know, the defences were formidable, the losses would be heavy all round, the defences came under attack from the sea and the air. The allied air forces strafed the reinforcement columns incessantly, with cannon and rocket fire. I believe we may have many, many casualties." He kissed her, then said, "I only stopped by to tell you the news. I have to go now, I have to move out of the city and assist with the communications as all hell has broken loose, telephone lines are down everywhere."

'The resistance, our people, my friends.' She thought.

She closed her eyes as he held her tight, the image of her, with Hans, baby Peter, walking in the sunshine under clear blue skies, grew stronger, she thought of meeting Ellen and Betty in the park for a picnic, the celebrations, the future.

He came home one evening, grinning. He said, "Start packing, you are moving to the North West coast well away from here. I requested you be moved, saying I would be able to concentrate better at my work knowing you were safe."

She moved off into the bedroom, he followed, holding Baby Peter. "You will like it there, fresh air from an incoming sea breeze. You will be staying at a farmhouse, which means fresh milk and eggs every day for you and Peter."

"And you, will you be safe?"

"Don't worry about me; we have a very deep bomb shelter.

You will like it there, I promise."

She opened a drawer, took out the package, looked at it, running her hand over it. "Are they are safe where they are?"

He remained silent; she searched his features, saw the despair there. She placed the package inside her suitcase, "Damn Nazi's, damn these people."

Garding.

Elfriede gazed out of the open window across Garding's coastal countryside, well away from the bombing, the city noise, the war, which she hoped would end soon. She spent most of her spare time walking with Peter. She went to the sideboard, picked up the package, clutched it to her bosom, held it as she imagined she would hold Ellen when they met once more.

After the Christmas celebrations, held to Elfriede's chagrin in the farmhouse of a staunch Hitler supporter where they now lived, Elfriede and Hans brought Peter to bed.

He looked at her. "The allies are getting closer, the so-called Third Reich is ending, and the Stauffenberg affair has left everyone nervous. I believe I may become caught up in this government's demise, retaliations by Hitler, if my department retreats to Berlin. I have had enough; I am going to desert at the earliest opportunity."

She looked at him, wide-eyed, pulling him to her. She looked round at Peter in his cot, fast asleep. "Where will you go, if they catch you they will shoot or hang you without any trial?"

He said as he looked around their cramped quarters, "I could hide here, behind the wardrobe, it's big enough." He indicated the huge wardrobe that contained not only their clothes, but some of the farmers 'Sunday best', arranged across the corner, behind the door to make more room. "There's space enough behind it, I can hide out there during the day when the need arises."

"What about these Nazi swine here, they might see you, and then what?"

He smiled, "They don't just barge in, do they, they always knock, and wait, so, there should be no problem there."

She looked at his eyes, they exuded confidence, she did not intend to put doubt into his mind, but she had to voice her own fears, "After you desert this will be the first place they will look for you, you cannot stay here."

He nodded, thought for a while. "You are right, but I won't come here, not straight away. I'll hide out somewhere, there are a few deserted barns around, they've been left derelict because of the constant floods, and I don't think the owners will be back, ever." He paused, then said. "Do you remember that barn where we sheltered from the rain during our cycle tour, that's where I'll hide for a while, but you mustn't come and visit me, you may be followed." He squeezed her gently, then kissed her softly. "Don't worry, everything will turn out fine, I'll fish and forage for food, there are enough small farm buildings and there's that stream not far from the barn where we went fishing once."

She smiled at the memory, "But we never caught anything."

"I'm not too sure, it probably got away."

Chapter thirteen.

Decisions.

As soon as he arrived home on leave Hans handed her a letter, she read it through and said, "Dresden?"

He nodded. "This is the opportunity I have been waiting for, it's a large department, and nobody there knows me. I will travel to Dresden and after booking in at my lodgings I will leave on the night train, and I'll come to you when it looks like it is safe to do so."

"Hans, I fear for Ellen and her sister's safety, do you think they have perished, I have heard people talking in the shelters about "extermination" is that true?"

"I don't know, it's not on our agenda, but I'm afraid it is most likely. Just keep on hoping; maybe they will survive this madness."

"Hope is all I have."

Dresden 1945.

Men, women and children crowded the pavement, running scared in the blackout as the sirens wailed.

As he reached the road, Hans managed to stop running just in time as a fire engine roared past, coming out of nowhere. He made his way across the road, dodging traffic, ignoring blaring horns, hurried towards the station entrance. He glanced at the station clock, realized his train left in half-an-hour. He had no idea where the ticket office was or the platform.

He found the ticket office easily enough, bought a ticket to Husum, boarded the evening train with time to spare.

As it pulled out of the station, he looked through the carriage window at the fires in the distance, heard more explosions as the bombers dropped their deadly cargo.

Soldiers checked his papers several times on the fully-packed night express; he produced his forged leave pass each time, pretending boredom, though remaining polite.

As the train pulled into Hamburg railway station, he kept a sharp lookout for any familiar faces, friends of Elfriede, kept his head down as passengers boarded the train.

He heard people talking about the British and the Americans bombing Dresden, he heard snatches of conversation from several

Air Force officers; they spoke of, firebombs and devastation. He decided he would have to change his plans in order to inform Elfriede of his survival.

Husum, North Germany.

After leaving the train at Husum during the twilight hours, he headed across country, using his compass, a small torch, a map he had acquired from the HQ map library, cutting across fields, avoiding the roads; hiding inside the hedgerows when necessary.

Shortly after noon, he found the small abandoned barn he and Elfriede had discovered, while on the cycling tour they had made that summer weekend.

Feeling safe, secure, with a comfortable bed of dusty straw, he ate from the pile of sandwiches he had prepared beforehand in the canteen, together with several boiled eggs from the two dozen he had appropriated, while drinking cold, sweet tea from his flask.

Tired from the long journey, he dozed off while waiting for the darkness to fall.

He awoke, looked at his watch, just past midnight. He cursed his foolishness, rose stiffly, gathering his things. He left, heading for the road, a wide well-worn earthen path spread unevenly with gravel, with high hedgerows on either side. He walked at a steady pace in near darkness, the only light a sliver moon, keeping his ears open for approaching vehicles wishing he had a bicycle right now.

After a few hours, peering occasionally into the distance behind him, hand cupped behind his ear, he spotted a faint light growing slowly brighter. Feeling exposed beneath the moonlit sky, he searched the hedge along the road. After finding a suitable gap he hunched down, waited, listening.

Soon, he heard the faint noise of steel crunching on gravel, together with the jingle of harnesses, the clopping of hooves growing louder.

Several minutes later a half-loaded hay cart rolled by, pulled by two horses with the driver seated on the cart front. The cart squeaked, groaned as it swayed over the uneven ground. He waited until it had passed, ran after it, climbed aboard through the open rear-end, hiding behind the stack of hay bales, peering ahead occasionally.

As the cart journeyed on, using his army compass, he took his bearings; found he was still heading in roughly the right direction.

***

Hours later, with the false dawn approaching to his right, he saw the lights of a farmhouse in the distance. Waiting for the appropriate moment, he left his mode of transport hiding behind some bushes at the roadside until the cart receded into the distance. He took out his compass, took his bearings once more. Pulling his overcoat collar up against the rising wind he strode off determinedly

Garding, once more.

Elfriede looked at the package, thinking of Ellen. She recalled the day she'd brought it to her; it was the day she'd decided to leave with Hans for Berlin, after that terrible bombing. She could still see the dead lying in the roadway, the children from the kindergarten, tattered bundles, laid out on the pavement.

She wondered what Ellen and Betty were doing now. She'd heard stories from her host, the Nazi adherent. How the Jews and other non-Aryans were put to work, forced to use toilets, wash their hands afterwards. She listened to him politely, as if agreeing with him.

She then recalled the last stories she had heard in the bomb shelters, horrific stories about gas chambers, mass graves, bonfires made up of bodies. Whatever Ellen and Betty's fate, she hoped this would be over soon, as Hans had said it would be.

While out walking with Peter that morning, she saw con-trails in the sky, heading east, she thought of Hans, "He'll be on his way to me by now, please God."

As soon as she returned entered their room, she placed Peter, half-asleep, in his cot, turned on the radio, keeping the sound to a minimum. She caught her breath as she heard the commentator, '...*this atrocity. In the city of Dresden the bombing continues, our brave defenders have brought down many of the enemy aircraft in flames. The British came in the early evening, dropping their deadly cargo on houses, schools, hospitals, and the railway station, their target, innocent German civilians. The fire-fighters are...*'

The room gyrated around her; she made her way to the bed, fell down upon it. "Hans, oh, Hans, where are you?" He'd said he was deserting his post as soon as he got there, but wouldn't be able to leave until night time because of the surprise Mosquito fighter nuisance raids.

The voice from the radio droned on, *'..have reported many casualties, most of them women and children, some of them taking refuge in a church, or a school. Nobody was spared in this cowardly onslaught. Dresden railway station is in ruins, locomotives and their carriages lie broken on the tracks, the passengers dead or dying, the police have taken...'*

She rose up, sobbing and turned the radio off. There came a knock at the door. She walked over to it, she opened it and saw the farmer's wife there her face ashen. "Have you heard, Frau Thunsdorff, the enemy are bombing Dresden, the British, and the Americans are intent on destroying one of our nation's most beautiful cities." She looked at Elfriede intently. "You have been crying, what is the matter?"

"My husband is stationed in Dresden."

The woman raised her hand to her mouth. "Oh, my goodness, I must tell my husband." With that, she hurried away.

She closed the door, went into the kitchen, she picked Peter up, as he stirred in her arms she held him firmly, she recalled her last night with Hans. "Oh, my darling Hans, where are you? Oh please God, keep him safe, out of harms way."

She had been dozing fitfully, lying on top of the bedcover, resting her back against the headboard. She sat up immediately at the noise, thinking it was Peter. She looked at the clock, ten-fifteen. She listened, there it was again, a light tapping sound on the bedroom window. She thought first about the farmer who was a stickler for blackout regulations, then about Hans leaving Dresden. "It's him, it's Hans, it has to be. Oh, God, let it be him."

She turned off the bedside lamp, slid off the bed, hurried over to the window, drew back the curtains. Her heart leaped as she saw him standing there in the moonlight, smiling.

She opened the window, he climbed inside wordlessly. She closed it, drew the curtains back in place, turned to him in the darkness. They embraced, kissed as if they had been apart for years. She whispered for fear of arousing Peter, "I feared you were dead, the British, they bombed Dresden, many hundreds were killed."

He whispered back hugging her to him, his heart beating in time with hers, "I was lucky; I left just as it started. I heard about it at the station in Hamburg, they said the whole city was ablaze, all those poor people."

He looked at her, his sadness showing in his features. Then he smiled and kissed her cheek. "I have missed you. I have been hanging around waiting for dark; I left the train at Husum as I couldn't risk getting off at Tönning or the station here and I walked most of the way. I stole a lift on a hay cart too. I had to come and see you in order to show you I'm still alive."

They kissed some more. After they broke off she said, "How long is this madness going to continue, the bombing, why are they doing it, a city bombed, why, will that end this stupid war?"

"I believe it is in retaliation. As for the war's end, I don't think we will have long to wait. The Americans are moving forward quickly, they and the British and their allies have a vast army, there is no stopping them, what with the bombings and the Mosquito raids, our army can only retreat or surrender, despite Hitler's demands that they fight to the last bullet. Hitler is insane, he has rages, ordering this, ordering that, his generals are at a loss, they daren't suggest surrender, he'd have them shot"

She rested her head against him for a moment. She said, "You look all in, you need a good night's rest, come to bed."

***

Several days later, the farmer knocked on the door as he usually did. Hans was already behind the wardrobe after they spotted the postal worker arriving.

She opened the door, the farmer stood there with his head bowed. He looked up as he held out a letter to her, his eyes watery, his face saddened. Realizing what it was, she gasped, placing a hand over her mouth.

He said quietly after she took the letter, "I sincerely hope it is not bad news, Frau Thunsdorff."

She was moved instantly by the man's simple compassion, even though she did not like him, then only because of his political attitude, as he was a hard worker who treated his family well, her and Peter with respect. She nodded her thanks, screwed her eyes up in pretended grief thinking. "I hope it is."

She thanked him quietly, closing the door. She opened the letter; after a few seconds she let out what she hoped was a convincing cry of grief.

Hans whispered softly as she stopped near the wardrobe, "What is it?"

She said in a wailing voice, "Oh, my poor husband, he's

dead, that dreadful bombing of Dresden, oh, dear God!"

Hans whispered, "Stop that or you will have me crying."

She sighed heavily, whispered, "Our luck, Hans, but other people's tragedy. Oh, my God, what a waste of human life." She wiped away a tear, said. "And all we can do is wait for this madness to end."

That evening as darkness came, Hans, as usual, climbed out of the bedroom window to stretch his legs for a couple of hours with Elfriede watching as he disappeared into the night.

During his absence, she took time to think of Ellen and her sister Betty, the opera lovers. They'd seen Verdi's Aida that evening on their first meeting; she'd taken a liking to both of them immediately. Betty the quiet one. Ellen, who, despite their situation, never failed to produce a smile. She thought sadly of her naivety, her faith in human nature, believing that good was in everybody.

She hoped fervently that Ellen and her sister were safe in some far distant place, far away from the bombing, not interned in one of those dreadful concentration camps.

She wondered what Ellen was doing at that moment. She looked forward to seeing her and her sister once more; she also looked forward to showing Peter off to them, smiling as she imagined their faces.

She thought sadly of Robert, her twin brother, of the last time she saw him. He had fallen in battle, just like thousands of others, just like Peter, the best man at their wedding. As far as she knew, her younger brother Hans was safe. She spoke a silent prayer for all the men and women who were fighting for freedom, all over the world.

Elfriede had lost so many friends in this war, some through the bombings. None of those who had left for Spain had returned. She had one last hope, that Ellen would return one day with her sister; she decided as soon as this mess was over she would contact the authorities.

She set the kettle on the stove next to the pan; she turned to a light knock on the door. She left the kitchen in a hurry and heard a familiar voice after asking, "Who is there?"

"Frau Thunsdorff, good evening, it is me, I have brought your milk and eggs."

Not forgetting her widow's face, she opened it. Her host stood there with a small urn half-filled with milk, the usual tiny basket with half-a-dozen eggs. "Good evening, Herr Bachmann," she said softly, "I thought it might have been someone from the military with news of my dear husband."

He handed over the goods in silence, she nodded her thanks. "Thank you very much, you are too kind." She smiled at him; she had grown to like him, despite his beliefs, for sometimes she felt sorry for her deceit.

He smiled back, "It is a pleasure, Frau Thunsdorff," he said, then he left.

She closed the door once more behind their all too frequent visitor, brought the milk and eggs into the kitchen. She was forever fearful that two-year-old Peter would one day call out to Hans as he lay hidden behind the wardrobe in the corner. She looked at the child, still curled up asleep in the tiny cot. She wondered what the future held for him.

British military zone.

Elfriede.

The war ended, peace returned to Europe.

Elfriede still had no news of Ellen and Betty, she thought often of the two sisters. Even though she received no news, she never gave up hope.

Hans came out of the bathroom, he saw Elfriede gazing out of their apartment window; she was clutching the package close to her chest. He approached her, laid a hand high on her shoulder, squeezed gently.

She felt the warmth of his hand as it caressed her tensed muscles; she hid her hanky from him, gazed round at him. He said softly, "You've been crying again haven't you?" She nodded, he continued, "You're still thinking about your two Jewish friends aren't you?"

She nodded once more, then turned away as a tear ran down her cheek. "I fear they are dead, Hans, you heard the rumours in the air raid shelters didn't you?"

"You keep on hoping my dear, maybe they will turn up."

"Hope is all I have; they say hope is what keeps people alive," she said, glancing down at the package, "This is my package of hope, for me, and for Ellen and Betty."

She rose, they embraced, standing there with their own

thoughts.

Elfriede spent all of her spare time listening to the radio, the English transmissions, as well as the German ones. The weeks, the months went by, she waited eagerly, impatiently, for news from any source. She decided after deliberation to ask the authorities.

One morning, leaving Peter with Hans she set off; as usual, she took the package with her.

***

After traipsing through the city, past the bombed factory buildings and housing, she approached the Allied HQ in the city centre. A young British soldier, wearing a red cap, stood on duty outside the door of the old building.

He eyed her suspiciously, as she approached him. "What do you want?"

She gave him a polite smile, answered in English. "I am trying to trace some people, is there someone I could talk to, one of your officers?"

"Who are they, these people?"

"They were Jewish," she added, "They were friends of mine; they were deported from Hamburg sometime in October 1941, I've been looking after their belongings until they return."

He shook his head. "We don't have that sort of information here. We don't know anything about missing persons or their belongings."

***

During the following years, Elfriede enquired relentlessly, hoping to hear something, anything of Ellen and Betty's fate, but the answer was nearly always the same. She resigned herself eventually to the fact that Ellen and Betty were dead.

***

The years passed by, then one day, because of Hans' ill health, Elfriede moved with him to Maennendorf at Zurichsee. Later in order to be near their grandchild, they moved to Weinheim.

As she grew older, whenever any of her grandchildren asked her about the package in her wardrobe, all the memories of that day came flooding back together with the tears.

***

On the 8th of July in 1994, at the age of 92, Elfriede passed on without knowing exactly what became of Ellen and her sister, believing they would only meet again in the afterlife.

The package lay unopened in her wardrobe until that day in Wheinheim, in December 2000.

Interlude.

Peter Thunsdorff's story.

*These are Peter Thunsdorff's own words translated by the authors with his permission.**

Elfriede and Hans' apartment,

Weinheim, Germany. 2000 AD.

I unlocked the apartment door and entered, greeted by the silence.

Standing in the hallway, I relished the familiar scent; I felt their presence still, even after their passing. With my father's recent death, and my mother's six years previous, I decided it was time to look things over before cleaning out the place.

I closed the door behind me and walked towards my mother's

room. The door swung open easily at my touch, and on entering, all the memories came pouring back. I heard her voice, reading to me from a children's book.

I visualised my mother at her writing desk, her pencil lying next to her open notebook. After all this time, everything was still in its place, her ruler, eraser, pencil sharpener, and dictionary, just as she liked it, and I realised my father had kept it this way.

I was a year old when my mother took me to meet my father at the railway station, where he yelled to her as he hurried to greet her: 'Damn that bomb - why didn't it work?' He was referring to the Stauffenberg assassination attempt on Hitler. Amazingly, neither of them was reported or arrested.

Gazing around at the family photos, the past years rolled by before my eyes, I heard children's laughter echoing in my mind, and I thought about the christenings, the birthdays, the holidays, and Christmas. I recalled my children searching in the local woods for chocolate eggs at Easter, then the wedding anniversaries, the tears, and finally both my parent's funerals.

With one last look around the room, I left the apartment, deciding it was time to sort things out, so in the next couple of weeks

I set to work.

One day, while sorting through the wardrobe in my mother's room, I came across a package tied up with string.

This same brown paper parcel had travelled with us every time we moved, which was often, and my mother always kept it close to her.

Curious, I opened the package and on seeing some of the contents, my mind went back to my childhood. This package had belonged to an old friend of my mother's, a woman who failed to return home from a long journey.

As I gazed at the articles before me I felt a shiver run down my spine, I felt like an intruder who had broken in on something and by opening the package destroyed something irreplaceable, like the extinguishing of a dying candle's flickering flame, blown out by some careless, inane gesture.

Replacing the contents carefully, I retied the package, which now felt much heavier, and took it home.

On my journey home, my mind travelled back to the stories my mother told me. I knew of her work with the German resistance during the Second World War, and I recalled the tale about the package.

I remembered amongst other things, my mother telling me of the time she took me to the railway station to meet my father, home on leave. It was the time of the failed assassination attempt on Hitler by Stauffenberg. My father had called out, "Damn that bomb – why didn't it work?"

It was a wonder that no one reported them, or had them arrested and thrown into prison, for in those times, dissention, speaking out against Hitler, could quite easily lead to a trip to the guillotine.

After arriving home from my late parent's apartment, I laid the package on the dining room table and my family gathered round. I told them what I knew about the package from what my mother had told me. My children nodded and one of them said sadly, 'Yes, that is the package that lay at the bottom of Gran's wardrobe, and when we went to fetch her something and asked her about the package she would start crying.'

I opened the package, measuring 30, by 20, by 15 centimetres, once more. Its contents included a small, embroidered tablecloth, several handkerchiefs, a half-dozen lace collars, an apron, a nightgown, a bar of soap, a flannel, a bottle of mouthwash and a small photo album, silent witnesses to one of the most terrible crimes in history.

I picked up the photo album and looked at my family as they gathered around and I opened it up. One of the photos could have been of Ellen herself at about the age of 30; it was a photo of a woman of rare beauty, her long dark hair tied behind her neck. The black and white photo showed her sitting on the grass in a wood somewhere, holding a wild flower, while wearing a long-sleeved light coloured dress, she was talking as she posed, probably to the photographer and she was happy, unaware of what lay before her.

I replaced the objects and tied up the parcel, and placed it somewhere safe, unsure what to do with the contents.

The package lay on a shelf for over four years, but I could not get it out of my head. Then one day I called on a friend of mine, Christian Petry, and told him all about the package and the story behind it.

"Christian, I think the best place for it would be the Jewish Museum in Berlin. I have not taken up contact with them as I am not sure of the proper procedure and I do not want the package to end up on a rubbish pile after all my mother's efforts."

Christian told me, "Write down the whole story and photograph the contents of the package, I have a good contact at the museum who would be very interested in your story, and the package, and I will see that it reaches him."

I thanked him and followed his instructions and two weeks later, I received a letter from the museum inviting me to bring the package to the museum, which I did at the earliest opportunity accompanied by my son Claudio.

I told my family, "If Ellen is still alive we can return the package to her or her descendants."

Peter Thunsdorff.

End of interlude.

Chapter fourteen.

Littmanstadt, January 1942.

Transfer.

The New Year arrived. Ellen and Betty worked in one of the other, smaller rooms in the clothing factory, sewing complete Wermacht uniforms together.

One day, at six o'clock in the evening, a kapo informed Ellen, Betty, and several other older women, after checking off their names on his clipboard, "You can return to your rooms, you are to remain there until called for tomorrow".

As he told them, Ellen noted a slight tremor in his voice; she wondered what had brought that on.

Back at their block, Ellen and Betty took the opportunity to shower undisturbed, under the steady ice-cold dribble; the only good side of this Spartan cleansing procedure was that it hardened them against the cold.

Betty called out as usual, "Ooh - aah, my God, this damn water's freezing."

Ellen smiled at her sister's antics under the rusty faucet, she called out, "Yes, it is rather invigorating, something I look forward to."

Betty laughed softly. "You, Ellen Kaempfer, are amazing, nothing ever gets you down, does it?"

"It is God's will, Betty I pray to him every night for our protection and well-being, he gives me strength."

She handed her sister a large piece of tattered towelling after she hurried to her, shivering, "Thank you sister for those words of endearment, now it's your turn."

While Ellen washed herself thoroughly Betty perused, 'What's in store for us now. What do you think, are we being promoted, as I'd rather have an extra ration card if they intend rewarding us, and a regular supply of potatoes."

"Yes, that would be nice, or we are to be promoted to street cleaners, gathering the dead."

Ellen finished her ablutions, turned off the water supply. She took the proffered towel, closed her eyes dreamily, breathed in through her nose, "Aaah, potatoes, boiled, mashed, or roasted, what I wouldn't give for one big fat juicy earth-apple." She opened her eyes, exclaiming, "I heard there was a riot earlier, because of a repeated potato shortage, is that true?"

"Yes, I heard that too, but it didn't amount to much."

"Why was that?"

"They shot the rioters."

"Oh dear!"

They finished dressing. Betty pulled on her overcoat, "Let's go shopping, sister dear, see if there are any 'big fat juicy potatoes' for sale."

***

She walked hand in hand through the pink and lilac fields of summer with Johannes, or 'Henness' as she called him, her husband of two days. They gazed at one another as they sat down by a bubbling stream, breathing in the scented air, then their heads turned as one, their lips touched.

Heaven, - she was in heaven – then she heard voices in the distance…

Ellen woke with a start, she sensed something, then she heard men shouting together with the cries of the building's occupants.

She heard the sound of leather-soled jackboots in the corridor.

The door burst open, kapos' and soldiers, German soldiers, came into in the room, shouting out orders, "Stand up, wake up you pigs, get up, move yourselves, quickly, quickly, move it now," while prodding Ellen and Betty's roommates none too gently with their rifle butts, as they lay in their bunks.

The kapo's added to the din, telling them, "Stand up you lot, you're moving out, pick up your things, quickly now."

Ellen scrambled to her feet before the rifle butts reached her and her sister; she climbed down, pulling Betty, who had long since given up complaining about her joints, to her feet. She was much lighter now, having lost a lot of weight, just like herself - so much that their clothes hung on them.

They pulled on their tattered footwear, picked up their meagre belongings. The kapo held Sarah and Ruth back.

Ellen and Betty left the room, stumbling as the soldiers shoved them along the corridor. Ellen looked up at a bright glass-covered rectangle above the stairway. "It's daytime, and the sun is up."

They both stumbled down the stairs with the others, the soldiers hounding them, shouting abuse. The came out onto the main street where they stood, waiting anxiously as a kapo read their names from a clipboard. An elderly woman called out in alarm, her arm outstretched, "God almighty, look."

In the light of day, the gathering crowd saw half-a-dozen tiny emaciated carcasses lying huddled together, either dead or dying, on the pavement near the corner of their building.

They saw another small ragged bundle, lying in the gutter on the other side of the road.

Ellen stared at her sister. "Oh my God, look at these poor children, what's the matter with them, where are they from?"

Betty brushed away a tear. "They had nobody to care for them; remember seeing those children chasing a rat? We haven't noticed these before as we leave for work in the dark and come back after the sunset."

Ellen, her eyes brimming, stared at one of the children nearest to them, a skeleton in rags, covered in parchment skin, barely alive. The child stared back, its large sunken eyes pleading, it raised a stick-like arm for a second before it dropped down. Her tears ran down her cheeks as she and Betty took a few steps towards it.

A kapo' stepped in front of them. "Leave it, it's no concern of yours, somebody else will take care of them, now get in line."

Ellen looked down the road at the sound of voices, she saw, not far away, a two-wheeled handcart, drawn by a group of men from the Ghetto, supervised by a Kapo as it came round the corner towards them.

One of the German soldiers called out to the group of elderly men and women, "Alright you lot, the show's over, now move it, onto the road, smartly now."

The group moved off, the cart passed by, going in the opposite direction.

Ellen gasped, her hand on her heart, she saw several hands and feet, some large, some small, hanging out over the rear, moving gently with the movement of the cart.

Another cart, its empty boards clattering, turned up from their end of the street; she watched in horror with others as the men from the ghetto flung or placed the small bundles from the roadside on to the cart in grim silence.

Then another cart rolled past them in the same direction as the first, like the first, it was fully loaded. Ellen faltered, pointed at a tiny hand groping in desperation under the weight of several large corpses. She received a sharp prod from a rifle butt, cried out, but not in pain, "That child, it is still alive."

The soldier, his rifle now lowered, growled, "Shut it Jew," pushing her forward, almost gently, with his hand, while averting his eyes from the macabre scene.

The human convoy, consisting of elderly or invalid people, young children, left the ghetto, crossed over the wooden junction, trudged towards a line of six canvas-covered lorries.

The kapo's assisted those too weak to climb into the back of the vehicles, filled to bursting, after which they secured the canvas coverings.

The trucks drove off.

They stood in the darkness, listening to the cries of children in the distance, screaming, some calling for their mothers, they heard babies crying too. Ellen reached out to Betty as she called out to her, "My God, what is happening here, Ellen, what are they doing?"

Ellen edged closer to her, trembling. "I believe this is the end." Then she started praying in Hebrew, joined by Betty and the rest of the lorry's occupants.

The truck stopped with a jerk. They heard the non-stop coughing, the hiss of steam, a train, waiting impatiently for its passengers.

The tailboard came down with a crash, the canvas curtain flew back. An officer, small, wiry with blond hair, screamed, "You lot, out, out now, go to the rear vehicles and help them."

Without hesitation, Ellen, Betty clambered down with the others, hurried to the rear vehicles.

They arrived at the last two trucks in line; saw several elderly women holding firmly onto babies as they clambered down from the trucks.

"You, get up there and get them out." At a word from the officer, one of the soldiers present handed his machine pistol to a comrade, climbed up inside the last vehicle, herded the occupants out.

Ellen looked up, saw small children and infants, standing there with grubby tear-stained faces, some crying, others with their visages distorted or frozen with fear. She moved forward with the others and helped them down. In the end, she found herself holding a skinny four-year-old girl.

She looked at Ellen. "I want my Mummy, where is she?"

Ellen looked at her, smiled. "Tell me child, what is your name?"

The child murmured, "Rebecca Kowalski."

"Don't worry Rebecca; I will take care of you until we find her." This quietened the child some and she laid her head on Ellen's breast.

Ellen turned to Betty as she carried an emaciated five-year-old boy, who unlike the rest was unnaturally quiet. "Now we are parents," said Betty.

An old man approached them, joined them as they walked on. They knew him from the factory, he was one of the cutters, Jacob Liebermann. He had a boy aged about nine with him, they asked him, "Do you know where they are taking us?"

Jacob picked the boy up, a thin child with dark rings around his eyes. "I have no idea, Madam, I hope to some place better than this hell hole."

Ellen looked at the boy. "Is he an orphan?"

"His parents were left behind." He looked around at the other people. "Haven't you noticed they are only moving the young and the very old?"

Betty asked, "Why is-."

A soldier called out, "Move yourselves you pigs, we haven't got all day."

Ellen looked at one of the soldiers, and he, for some reason, turned his head away, refusing to meet her gaze.

The officer in charge screamed, "Move out, board the train, now."

Ellen looked at her sister who glanced back in concern. She felt a certain discomfort, as the soldiers escorted them in an unnatural silence, to a long line of cattle wagons, the only noise the tantrum-like screaming of the officer.

The group spread out, they climbed aboard with dozens of others by way of a gangplank. The strong smell of disinfectant invaded her nostrils as she entered the cattle truck. She sighed with relief as she saw numerous bales of straw, several water-filled buckets.

Together with her sister, she sat down on a small mound of straw, nursed the girl, enjoying its need for comfort, pretending it was her own.

The cattle truck, half-full, swayed, groaned, the planking creaked, complaining as the train, a relict from days gone by, trundled over numerous points.

At one point, Ellen heard the distant droning sound of aircraft engines. As the sound drew nearer, the carriage lurched, the brakes screeched, throwing those standing off balance.

She heard soldier's voices ringing out in panic, their voices receding into silence.

Someone called out, "Why have we stopped?"

"I can hear aircraft."

"I hope it's not the Yanks, they attack trains y'know."

Aircraft droned overhead, women sobbed, men cursed, children called out.

Silence.

"They're flying away from us," said Jacob

"Thank God," said Betty

After the sound of aircraft faded into the distance, they heard the soldier's voices once more, this time filled with relief, seconds later the train started off once more, bumpers clanking, carriages shunting, shaking.

A while later, Ellen heard the crump of bombs exploding in the distance; the soldiers had left them at the mercy of the enemy bombers, but lucky for them, they had more important targets than a rickety old steam train pulling dilapidated cattle trucks.

The child, slumbering peacefully in her arms murmured, "Mummy."

Ellen pulled her closer and said in Yiddish, "Sleep my Angel, sleep on, you are safe with me."

Chapter fifteen.

Chelmno.

Ellen awoke with some of the others. The train had stopped once again. This time she heard men's voices, outside, talking, conversing in a normal manner.

The door slid back, waking those who had slept on, some of

the children called out in fright. Everyone's gaze turned to the sun's rays streaming in, warming the air in the unusual silence.

Soldiers called out to them, "Everyone out, come on, lively now."

Rebecca stirred in her arms; she opened her eyes. "Where are we, where is my mummy?"

Ellen sat her up; pulled several strands of straw from her hair. "I don't know, we have stopped, and we have to go outside."

A soldier pointed, saying, "Assemble at those lorries waiting over there."

They climbed down, joined the rest of the group as they walked unhurriedly towards a row of army trucks, accompanied by soldiers. They boarded the vehicles with their help, took their places on the seating.

As the last tailboard closed, the convoy moved off.

Ellen peered through a hole in the canvas, Rebecca asked her, "Where are we, are we going home?"

Ellen pulled her closer. "We are travelling through open countryside. I can see cattle; maybe we are going to work on a farm."

After a while the vehicles stopped.

Ellen rose with Rebecca up into her arms. She went over to Betty holding the little boy she had taken into her care.

The boy looked around calmly.

Ellen smiled at him, he looked back at her plaintively.

She waited for him to say something, saying to Betty, "He seems to be taking it rather well, but he isn't all that receptive is he?"

Betty said quietly, "He's deaf, thank God."

Ellen looked once more at the boy; this time she saw the pain, the despair in his eyes as he stared back at her. She said without turning away, "Yes, but he's not blind."

Betty hugged the boy to her, "It would be a blessing if he were."

"Yes, but then he would be shot, just like that poor girl, and her mother."

The tailgate lowered slowly, voice interrupted their melancholy, "Will all occupants please leave the vehicles and form a line outside."

Encouraged by the friendly tone, they climbed down with the rest of the passengers, lining up by the lorries in the powdery snow.

Soldiers of the SS stood around in small groups, several of them were armed, most of them were smoking, or chatting, laughing with one another. None of the soldiers seemed concerned with the vehicle's occupants.

While holding onto Rebecca, Ellen took a few steps forward, peered past a dilapidated wooden shed. She saw, not far away, a large old-fashioned building, partly visible behind a line of trees.

She looked around as a Kubelwagen rolled up a road leading from the direction of the building, coming to a stop before the crowd. Ellen stepped back in line.

A smartly-dressed army officer greeted them as he stood up inside the vehicle, "Welcome to Chelmno," he called out, finishing with a smile.

One of the elderly women asked him politely, "Excuse me sir, what is this place, what are we to do here?"

The officer indicated behind him, "The building visible in the distance is Castle Chelmno, a recreation camp, a nursing home so to speak, it has been prepared especially for you and the children. Doctors will examine you before appointing you your tasks, light work only of course, and those who are in no condition to perform any of these menial tasks will each be cared for by a trained nurse."

He paused as he gazed at the crowd then said pleasantly, "In a short while, I would like you all to walk in an orderly fashion with the guards to the building behind me. From there you will journey in special trucks to a public bathing facility. After you have washed and bathed in hot water, you will be given new warm clothing and footwear, and then you will be fed." He turned to an army officer who had travelled with the train, "Is that the lot, Jochen?"

The man answered tiredly, "Yes, for the time being," and turned away without further comment and boarded the leading lorry.

The officer climbed down from his vehicle; he motioned to two dozen policemen armed with machineguns, they walked with him as he inspected the newcomers. Walking past them, he pointed to half-a-dozen men, the fittest it seemed. One of them was Jacob Liebermann. They marched away with the officers, boarded two canvas-covered lorries, which promptly drove off.

Ellen, looking at Betty in concern said, "I wonder where they are going."

"They are going on ahead to run hot baths for us."

Ellen laughed softly along with others, then turned to Betty saying, "Sometimes you go too far with your droll levity, but this time I believe you could be right."

The officer shouted out to them, waving in a friendly fashion, "Everybody move out, sharply now." Then he added to those nearest to him, his eyes twinkling as they smiled back at him, "You don't want to miss lunch do you?"

The crowd of people moved off in an orderly fashion towards the trees, the building beyond beckoning them, chatting cheerfully.

Betty said quietly to Ellen, "Can you believe this?"

"I keep pinching myself to see if I'm dreaming, isn't this wonderful."

Betty looked at her sister, then fell silent.

***

Seated in the leading vehicle, on his way back to the train station, Lieutenant Jochen Biedermann lit his pipe, turned to the driver who asked him, "Is that place really a nursing home for Jews, sir?"

Biedermann turned away, his features void of expression, "Yes, of course it is."

***

After a lengthy walk, the crowd arrived at an old manor house. They saw a line of men and women standing outside, dressed in white, quietly observing them, some of them smiling.

Someone in front said quietly, "They must be the doctors and nurses."

Another said, "I can smell food, real food, oh, my God, real food at last."

Ellen breathed in through her nose, her mouth watered suddenly. She swallowed, she could smell boiled potatoes, green cabbage, roast beef. She saw several open windows in the building, heard the noise of pots and pans, clanging, rattling loudly. She turned to Betty, eyes wide. "I wonder what our rooms will be like; they probably have hot running water and beds, soft beds with clean sheets."

Betty remained silent her features expressionless.

Ellen looked up to the sky, took a deep breath, sighed softly, letting the air out slowly. "How quiet it is here, just the place for peace and serenity."

"It's a little too quiet for me," said Betty.

"Why do you say that?"

She shrugged. "I don't know, Ellen," she said, "It's just a feeling I have, as if this is as far as we go."

Ellen stared at her sister, then turned away as the officer pulled up in his Kubelwagen, calling out to them as he pointed to his right, "Be so kind as to enter the building into the hallway and remove all your clothes. New clothing will be available for all, shoes too, at the bathing facility. After that please proceed into the cellar, my men will show you the way. At the other side of the building you will find transport waiting for you in specially heated trucks, they are your transport to the bathing facility, the journey may be a little cramped, as the proper transport was destroyed in a bombing raid, but you will arrive in no time at all."

A young police officer left the line of people waiting by the building. He approached the other, "I hope none of the trucks blow up like that last one, what a mess that was. Lange will have our guts for garters when he returns."

The other replied, "Yes, he wrote complaining about the danger, they assured him these were of an improved quality and they have lighting."

"Kohl told me you instructed him to put all of this lot into the three trucks?" He indicated the waiting crowd with a flick of his gloved hand, "You'll never get all them all inside three trucks, Karlchen, there are far too many."

"Yes I will, Dieter my darling boy, just you watch me, it is better this way too, more expedient if you think about it, the results of which I will include in my report."

The other raised an eyebrow, shook his head, saying, "A bottle of Claret says you won't get every single one of them in."

"You're on, my boy; Kohl knows what he is doing, as he used to work as a packer for a removal firm."

"How appropriate."

***

Ellen and Betty walked with the rest of the crowd into the building. In the huge hallway, they divested themselves of their clothing, then walked with the crowd towards the stairway indicated by the guards, then entered the cellar.

Rebecca whispered to her, "Where are we going, I'm cold?"

Ellen picked her up, pressed her shivering body to hers, "We are going for a bath; maybe we will have a swim or a shower. When we come back, we will have new clothes and receive a hot meal.

Maybe later your mother and father will join us." The child remained silent, snuggled her thin body against hers.

Ellen had visions of them all, splashing, cavorting in a huge steaming pool, laughing, calling out to one another. Her daydream faded as they walked through the cellar along a dimly lit passage.

After climbing a stone stairway, they left the building, walked outside into the sunlight. A long ramp stretched out before them, they saw three vehicles backed close up to it. The vehicles were large plain metal vans, their rear doors open, each with a railed access ramp leading into it.

They were divided into groups of 35 to 40 by one of the policeman, moving people around until he was satisfied.

Ellen and Betty found themselves with others by the third truck. As he gave the word, they hurried inside grateful to be out of the cold.

The policemen called out, encouraging them to assist them in their task as they forced an elderly woman carrying a baby, into one of the trucks. A number of them had long sticks, they were wielding them as if waiting for an excuse to use them. One of them called out, "Raise your arms above your heads then you will have more room."

Another called out, "As soon as we close the doors we can turn on the heating."

They pushed at the people in the doorways, using their sticks gently but forcibly, packing their human cargo tighter together, ignoring the cries of indignation.

Inside their truck, Ellen had trouble breathing, Rebecca whimpered until she lifted her clear of the crush.

Then the light grew dim as the door closed.

Ellen asked, "What are we standing on?"

A woman called out, "A bloody uncomfortable grill."

Somebody remarked, "It must be for the heating."

"I hope so, I'm bloody freezing."

"Why are we packed in so tight, I can hardly breathe?"

"I don't like this," said Betty

Ellen held Rebecca firmly by her thighs, daydreamed once more. 'A warm bed, clean clothes, and real food, why were so many people so cruel to us, and the others, hitting us and stealing our possessions, why didn't they bring us here in the first place, then there would not have been so many deaths and misery?'

Her mind turned to the dead children in the Ghetto, the

people in the cattle truck on their first journey; she said a silent prayer for them. As she finished praying, she heard somewhere in the truck a child asking, "Why is it so dark in here?"

A woman's voice answered, "Don't fret; they'll probably put the lights on when we start the journey."

They heard someone shouting angrily outside, hurried footsteps, then the cab door slammed shut. A light above them came on, a woman called out, "See, what did I tell you."

Ellen sighed, the air inside the vehicle was warmer now because of the tightly packed bodies, but it was a little stuffy.

Rebecca was quiet, she listened, heard her breathing deeply, she took hold of her hand, gripped it firmly.

She heard the other cab doors closing, then she heard a whistle blow. She turned to where Betty stood. "We are on our way; at last a better place to live and enjoy freedom once more."

Then the vehicle's motor started…

***

The two officers walked towards their Kubelwagen, the junior one said, "Is Medoc alright with you my dear?"

"The 1905 if you don't mind, we can share it in the bath

together."

"As you wish, Karlchen."

The Woods near Chelmno.

Jacob Liebermann looked at the old men packed together in the back
of the truck; he recognised several from the ghetto, nodded to them,
like them, not knowing what to say. He was, like the others,
surprised by the reception, which to him, now seemed more like
deception.

The ones unknown to him also sat in silence, their features
set, eyes hard.

He felt his shins where the leg-irons, fitted before they set
off, had bitten into his skin. He asked one of the strangers seated
near the tailboard, "Where are we going, are we going to the same
place as the others, why are we chained up?"

The man regarded him coldly.

A voice from the front said loudly, "Yes, we have special
work to do. When we get there just do as you're told."

Jacob looked across at his roommate from the ghetto, he just
stared back, shrugged, his eyes without expression.

After a short bumpy ride the trucks stopped, the tailboards dropped down. The man next to him climbed down, Jacob and the rest followed. A dozen police officers climbed out of the second vehicle, started shouting out orders as they herded the twelve men to a snow-covered clearing. In the middle was a long trench about two metres deep. The group separated, the newcomers from the old.

Two of the policemen handed pliers, cloth bags to six of the men saying to Jacob's group, "You will wait here, and you will keep quiet."

Jacob saw three medium-sized vans approaching, a few of the men murmured in consternation, one of the men said, "What are those vehicles for, what are they doing here?"

Someone else said, "They contain your travelling companions."

The man said, "I thought they were going to a bathing facility, that's what the officer said."

A policeman, guarding them, turned angrily, swinging his machine pistol in their direction. "You lot, shut your mouths or you'll lose your teeth the hard way."

The vans pulled up, parked in a line close to one another, the motors dying, the rear doors facing the waiting group. The men spread out behind the vans, the new ones following the other's lead.

A Kubelwagen arrived with the two officers who watched as two of the men opened the rear door of the last van in line, they swung them back quickly.

Jacob saw the occupants standing naked, huddled together, fear frozen on their faces, then slowly one of them, an old man, moved, toppled forward stiffly out of the truck. As if this was a signal, the row of bodies fell forward with him, landing heavily on the snow-covered ground, followed immediately by the next row, which was followed by the others until the naked bodies of men, women, children, toddlers even, lay piled up at the rear of the vehicle.

Jacob, in his naivety, feared some mishap had taken place with the first van, until the next van doors opened. His naivety left him as he realised they had been duped, the occupants had been murdered somehow on their way here. The occupants packed tightly inside at first refused to budge, until the front row fell forward as one, after which the rest of the van's inhabitants, suffocated by engines gases, pumped into the rear by way of a special exhaust system, fell, or rolled out of the vehicle.

The same happened with the third van.

Jacob stared in horror at the piles of naked bodies.

The man next to Jacob retched dryly, another one passed out. Jacob turned to one of the others and asked, "What do we do, bury them?"

The man, aged about seventy said, "Yes, we dug the grave yesterday." He produced the pliers saying, "But first we have to remove any gold teeth we find." He stepped forward to the pile, grabbed a child's body, flung it, as if it were a rag doll, to one side, then he grabbed a woman by the wrist, pulled her clear of the others, rummaged in her mouth, said to Jacob, "Come here with the bag."

As Jacob neared him, he poked the pliers inside the woman's mouth. Jacob heard a sickening tearing sound as the tooth, a molar with its gold filling, left its socket. After he had finished extracting several more, the man turned to Jacob, who stood there as if in a dream, bag in hand, dropping bloodied teeth inside it.

Jacob watched as his companion repeated the action with most of the adult bodies. Soon the bag was full, after which he approached one of the guards who gave him a fresh bag in exchange. As he came back, Jacob said, "I can't go on, I feel sick, and if my stomach wasn't empty I would throw up."

They both looked around at the sound of a pistol shot, they watched as one of the men who had fainted earlier, fell, pole-axed, to the ground. The man said, "Do you want to finish up like him, cos' I don't? Now take the bag or I'll do you in myself." The man pushed the bag into his hands, Jacob complied, afraid.

After they cleared the pile of bodies away from the trucks, the men climbed inside the vehicles, threw the rest of the carcases out onto the snow.

The work continued.

It seemed the sky wept that day in penance for what they were doing. The rain poured down steadily, as if attempting to wash away Jacob's sins, sins of the other's.

The whole action, watched over carefully by the police guards, took over four backbreaking hours. When they had finished, the rain ceased. They handed the bags with the gold teeth to an NCO.

Jacob heard the senior officer call out from the shelter of the trees, "Bring the bodies to the pit, and be quick about it."

Jacob, his senses numb, his mind shocked, bewildered, looked around in a daze at the bodies lying on the snowy ground. He saw the little boy he had carried from the truck lying there, his eyes, mouth, wide open. He raised his hands to his face, hoping to still the tears running down his cheeks, sobbing quietly as he stumbled forward, slipping, sliding over the muddy ground with the others.

They dragged or carried the corpses to the two-metre deep mass grave, dropped, rolled, or threw them in, without ceremony, without a thought, then hey came to the bodies from the last truck.

Jacob looked at the naked bodies of old men, women, little children in shame as he carried out his onerous task. He looked down at one of the women lying there, he recalled he had spoken with her earlier, he knew her from the Ghetto, from the clothing factory where he had worked. She'd carried a child to the train, a girl it was, her sister had a deaf boy with her; now she lay there, her gentle features unmarred by death, still holding the little girl's hand.

The child appeared to be asleep, untroubled just like the woman. He pried the woman's hand loose with some difficulty, he envied them, gone on to a better world that he now found himself in.

He carried the child to the grave, laid her gently on top of several bodies. He carried the woman together with his roommate, laying her carefully next to her, then carried on.

With all the bodies in the grave, the men filled it in, working from one end to the other. As they reached the last six metres of open grave, the senior officer called out, "Stop, stop now, you must be very tired, stop, and rest for a while."

As the men turned away from their grisly work, stretching their aching backs they found themselves facing the junior officer with an array of police officers pointing their machine pistols at them.

The last word Jacob heard was - "Fire."

Chapter sixteen.

Aftermath.

Minden 1945.

Nineteen-year-old Elke Dern watched her mother in the mirror as she plaited her long blond hair, she fidgeted, eager to go out with her girl friends. The war was over, the American soldiers were everywhere. "Mother, do hurry, Birgit and the others are waiting."

Her mother smiled as she tied the last bow, she knew she was off to chat with the American soldiers. She asked tentatively, "Do you think maybe you could bring some chocolate back with you, and maybe a few cigarettes, for Papa?"

Fate had been gracious to them, her father, a fireman had survived the bombings, one of her brothers was now home from hospital, after losing an arm fighting in Russia, the other was in a British prisoner of war camp in the north of England, the youngest, Dieter, was laying telephone cables with the military.

"I'll see what I can do." She hesitated, said, "May I bring a friend home with me?"

Her mother gasped. "You mean an American soldier? I don't think Papa would approve."

"You'll like him, he's nice, his name is Robert, he speaks German, and he is a junior officer, an interpreter."

Her mother pondered for a while, watched as her daughter inspected her handiwork. "I will ask Papa, if he says yes, then you may. But I am not promising."

She gave her mother a kiss, said, "Okay, I'll see you later."

She hurried down the stairs, out the front door then ran down the street towards the market place where her friends were waiting. They would practice their English on the American soldiers, "Ami's" they called them, they would giggle at the young soldier's attempts at German, mostly at the wrong pronunciation.

Elke, at seventeen, was, like her friends, almost the same age of most of them, nineteen being the youngest. The soldiers would give her, the other girls' chocolate, chewing gum, as they did the younger children. They didn't seem any different from the people she knew, why, some of them even had German names.

One of them, Birgit's friend, named Charles, Charlie, or

"Chuck" for short, told them that his last name was Scharschmitt. He told her his grandfather had left Germany for America as a young man, had decided to keep the family name as he was proud of being German, was even prouder that his grandson was fighting fascism in order to free his former homeland.

She rounded the corner; saw them, three of her friends. Robert was with them. As she reached them, he took her quickly to one side. "Hi, Elke, how are you?"

She saw his troubled features. "I'm fine; I spoke to my mother about us-." She hesitated. "What's wrong, what has happened?"

He took a deep breath. "I can't tell you anything only that you and your family, in fact the whole city is in for a terrible shock, I would like to be there with you, but my CO forbade it."

Her body tensed, was he leaving, going home, so soon! No it couldn't be that. She clutched his uniform sleeve. "What is going to happen to us, is it bad, the Russian soldiers, are they…?"

He shook his head. "No, nothing like that, it's something everybody must see. It's a film show, about what the Nazis did to people. I can't tell you more, I just wanted to say that everybody must go and see this." He paused for a moment. "I, I hope this doesn't spoil our relationship as I would like very much to see you as often as I may. I will be there, in the park on Friday evening at the usual time; if you don't come I will understand." She regarded his worried features as he continued. "You will receive notification and – I am so sorry, I- ." He looked down, then he turned, hurrying off towards his jeep.

Her friends approached her questioning her. She repeated everything he told her.

The next day, she, her mother, along with many others from their part of the city of Minden, by order of the military, attended a film show given by the Americans at the Scala Cinema, told that refusal to attend would mean the loss of their ration cards.

She'd heard of the concentration camps where Jews, enemies of the state, undesirables worked under duress. She'd heard rumours of gassing, she assumed they must have been criminals, murderers.

Then, sitting there, in the darkness, she, with her mother, saw man's inhumanity to man. They realised the stories they had heard, which they thought were just stupid tales from people who were only after attention, were, after all this time, all too true.

They saw the starving children, the gibbets, the hanging bodies, the mounds of naked cadavers, men, women, children, even babies, then they saw the uncovered mass graves filled with hundreds of corpses.

She saw along with the rest of the audience the bodies piled onto handcarts, the gas chambers, appearing like communal showers, ovens, row upon row of ovens, some of them with their chimneystacks still smoking, their one purpose, to burn the corpses.

They saw the living skeletons, dressed in ragged, dirty, striped clothing, some of them stone-faced, some of them smiling, glad to be alive.

The film lasted almost an hour in which the initial shock wore off changing to horror. Then the horror changed to tears.

After the film show ended, Elke left the cinema with the others, crying along with her mother, to the astonishment of the waiting crowd outside on the streets. She was ashamed of what she had seen, she felt betrayed by her own country.

That evening she met Robert in the park, he listened to her, consoling her.

The next day she brought him to her home to meet her

family, without asking her father's consent.

Elke and Robert married six months later and left for America some time later.

Epilogue.

Weinheim 2005

On their return home from Berlin, Peter Thunsdorff told his family what he and Claudio had discovered at the museum: "After we handed the package over with all the details, we were invited to tour the Museum and we searched for the name Ellen Kaempfer. We found out she was born on the 11th of January in 1894. She was married and then later divorced in 1938. Her maiden name was Holstein and we found she had an elder sister and her name was Betty Holstein, single, born on the 17th of June 1884, they both worked for a steel manufacturing firm, Coutinho Cara and Co, and they lived in an apartment block in Hamburg at Eichenstrasse 22. They were living there at the time of their deportation to Lodz in Poland in October 1941."

He paused; adding after taking several deep breaths, "Then on or around April the 5th 1942; they were taken along with others from the Ghetto in Lodz to the extermination centre at Chelmno, where they were brutally murdered, their bodies buried in a mass grave."

End.

Thank you for purchasing this book. The authors would appreciate a comment relating to the book, how you felt while reading, after you read it and how it affected you.

Historical facts.

Killer Vans.

The following is a translation of a letter to SS-Obersturmbannführer Walter Rauff, referring to the alterations made to the vans used to gas Jewish men, women and children and transfer their bodies to the

woods near Chelmno for burial in a mass grave.

(Cold and dispassionate as if he was referring to alterations to a

garden fence.)

June 5, 1942.

From Willy Just.

RE: Technical alterations to the special vehicles already in

operation and those in production.

(1) Since December 1941, for example, 97,000 have been

processed using three vans without any faults developing in the

vehicles. The well-known explosion in Kulmhof must be treated as a

special case. It was caused by faulty practice. Special instructions

have been given to the relevant offices in order to avoid such

accidents. The instructions were such as to ensure a considerable

increase in the degree of security.

Further operational experience hitherto indicates that the following

technical alterations are appropriate....

2) The vans are normally loaded with 9-10 people per square meter. With the large Saurer special vans this is not possible because although they do not become overloaded their manoeuvrability is much impaired. A reduction in the load area appears desirable. It can be achieved by reducing the size of the van by c. 1 meter.

The difficulty referred to cannot be overcome by reducing the size of the load, for a reduction in the numbers will necessitate a longer period of operation because the free spaces will have to be filled with CO. By contrast, a smaller load area which is completely full requires a much sorter period of operation since there are no free spaces.....

3) The connecting hoses between the exhaust and the van frequently rust through because they are corroded inside by the liquids which fall on them. To prevent this, the connecting piece must be moved so that the gas is fed from the top downwards. This will prevent liquids flowing in.....

(6) The lighting must be better protected against damage than hitherto....

It has been suggested that lighting should be dispensed with since they are allegedly never used. However, experience shows that when the rear door is closed and therefore when it becomes dark, the cargo presses hard towards the door and this makes it difficult to latch the door. Furthermore, it has been observed that the noise always begins when the doors are shut presumably because of fear brought on by the darkness.

Just, Willy.

Also by Ellen Dudley and T. J. Edison.

For all the Wrong Reasons.

This is not a romance, nor is it a love story; but, it is about love, how it held people together, gave them hope for a better future in a time of want, of war, of separation and sometimes, despair.

Foreword.

Have you ever asked yourself why countries go to war?

The answer is obvious.

For all the wrong reasons, that's why.

But then again, are there any right reasons?

Eva van de Leyhn, an American woman of Jewish-Catholic heritage falls in love and marries a German engineer and journeys with him to his home in Dresden, there she meets his family. At the outbreak of war, she refuses to leave her husband and remains in the family home. He goes off to war, and after the birth of their child and her husband's heroic death she leaves Dresden on the night of the 1945 bombing and joins her in-laws at their new home.

Then one misty morning whilst riding in the local forest she stumbles upon a terrible secret.

Taking Care of Timothy.

By

Ellen Dudley.

How difficult is it to escape from one's past life when we are not aware of the dangers that pursue us over distance and time; what are the chances of survival without the trust and help of strangers?

And, how strange that malevolence can sometimes change our destiny for the better, despite further antagonistic intentions.

***

CPSIA information can be obtained at www.ICGtesting.com
Printed in the USA
BVOW06s2205050916

461216BV00023B/195/P